Hello Happiness

by

CARRIE McGOVERN

Dedication

I dedicate this book to my husband, who has supported me and has had to put up with my craziness for nearly two decades. Love you!

Chapter One

Emma

What has my life actually become? I'm hurtling towards 40 and I don't even know if I actually have a real name. I have all kinds of titles, Mum generally, but it usually has a drawn out 'uuu' sound. I also get MOTHER, if they want something or I'm being embarrassing, which happens a lot. Sometimes I just have to breathe the wrong way in their direction for that title.

I am also the washer of all clothes, which includes picking up said washing off the floor and putting it into the wash basket that's less than a metre away. Taxi driver to events, sporting fixtures or general socialising meetups, none of them my own. This job also means having to drop everything at a minute's notice to accommodate said events. Also known as general dog's body, encyclopaedia and giver of advice that is immediately discarded. Then, when that advice was not heeded and things go a bit wrong, I am also to blame for not giving the advice that they dismissed. I can't win! It's probably my own fault though for wanting a quiet life. I am raising the men of the future, but I have become the epitome of the 1950s housewife. So I apologise to my kids' future partners for that.

My phone rings and the caller ID flashes up on screen. It's the school. Of course it's the school, it's always the bloody school! Which child is it now? I know the answer to that one too, it's always the same child, same issues, different day.

I answer it, knowing we'll have the same conversation as we always do.

"Hello Ms Lowther, it's nothing to worry about, but Joshua isn't feeling well again."

Of course he's not, this kid is allergic to school. But of course, he doesn't need to attend because he knows everything better than the rest of us. In his extensive 15 years on the planet, he has the full knowledge of life stored in that man-boy brain of his.

"Hi Claire," I answer, "you may as well call me Emma, we speak more often than I speak to my family." She knows the score as well as I do. If I don't come and collect him, we'll both be harassed until I do. "Do you need me to collect him? I take it he's far too ill to stay in school?"

She lets out a sound that's half laugh, half frustrated grunt. "If you don't mind, I'll see you soon."

Oh, why would I mind? It's a good job I'm not a high-flying career woman, the amount of times I get pulled out of work for one reason or another. Not to mention special assemblies, sports days, school plays, presentation evenings, parents evenings... The list is never-ending.

After I had the kids, I went back to a boring admin job and kind of never really got out of that rut. I work flexible hours, so I come in early to make sure everything gets done before I get pulled away. And I always get pulled away. I am the proverbial doormat of my family. And yet still my husband left me, for the clichéd younger model, office secretary, although he won't admit it.

The divorce was somehow my fault, as everything always is. I don't remember why, maybe I didn't cook him the right meals, I didn't answer to his every need, or I'd *let myself go* or whatever. Apparently I didn't pander to his every need anymore, which I actually did, so it was all a bit confusing. He said I wouldn't have sex with him anymore, but in the same breath said he didn't find me attractive. And ever since then I have been an emotional punchbag for David. Whenever he gets the opportunity, he tells me what a rubbish job I did of raising the children, being a wife and that my life sucks. Never in those words though. They come as a back handed compliments like *At least that dress doesn't make you look fat,* or *If only we could all spend our weekends watching Netflix.* There must be more to my life than this!

It's a good job I am getting one of my regular therapy sessions this weekend. It's not conventional therapy. It's me and my four friends trying to put the world to rights after a few cocktails. It'll most definitely cost less too.

I pack my desk up without a word and make my way out of the office, giving Beth a quick wave on the way. The office has not changed in the past decade – well probably even longer than that. There are peeling posters of trucks on the walls, bleached by the sunlight and with a registration plate that predates my teenage kids. My desk still has a diary in the drawer from the year 2000, probably the same year Windows was installed on the computer I use. I don't think anyone even notices I'm leaving anymore. I'm pretty much invisible to everyone until they want something.

My friends are the only bit of sanity I have, and they have seen me through all kinds of crises and mini-meltdowns. And I have picked them up off the floor when needed, physically and metaphorically. They are a mix of everything and I live vicariously through some of them. We are a mismatched bunch. You'd never really put us all together as a group of friends, but I think that's how it works so well. We've been this dysfunctional little family of five for over a decade now.

Sammy is my oldest friend in the group. We met at university, so we go back a long way. She knows a lot of incriminating stuff about me, but I know more about her. We have to be friends now so that the other one doesn't spill all our secrets. In all honesty, although we don't talk all the time, we get together and pick up like we were never apart. If I'm ever arrested, at least I know my best friend-come-lawyer will save the day.

Sammy moved to Edinburgh after university to practice law at some hotshot firm. She's the one with the taste and the money, partly because she has an amazing career but also because she never had kids. God, I really envy her sometimes, being able to do things without notice. She can go on holiday when she wants and not when the school term dictates. She sees who she wants to, goes out for a drink or to dinner when she feels like it. Sometimes on the way home from work on a scorching hot day, I am itching to be sitting outside in the sun with a glass of something, but no, I carry on and get home to be the responsible parent. Again.

Don't get me wrong, I love my kids. But life is so tiring at times, and I'm not always that keen on being a parent. I suppose the label *single parent* doesn't really shed light on my situation, because Joshua and Noah's dad is still in the picture. He takes the boys off my hands and over to his every now and again, sometimes he may as well not even bother.

We are heading up to see Sammy this weekend. She's hosting this time, which means it's going to be wild. She's flashing her cash and renting a swanky apartment for us all, and we'll be visiting fancy restaurants and cocktail bars until she kills us with alcohol poisoning. Thank goodness this only happens once a year. Nights nearer to home are so much more tame in comparison, just a few drinks at the Dog and Swan.

Chapter Two

It's Saturday lunchtime and the four of us are standing in Edinburgh Waverley station, waiting for Sammy to tell us where we're going. The journey is only an hour and a half by train – enough time to have finished off two bottles of prosecco between us.

She's late as usual and not answering her texts, so we hang around, looking out of place, four middle-aged mummies on tour. Beth has been given a weekend pass from her husband. He didn't have a choice and he would have let her come, no questions asked, but she still has mummy guilt for leaving her kids. All he has to do is keep them alive for a little over 24 hours, but she has rung Steve approximately 14 times in the time it has taken us to get here.

I sometimes feel sorry for Steve. He's a great guy and more than capable of being a dad, but Beth hates not being in control. Added to that, he's just a typical bloke who doesn't think before he acts. It's usually something nice he is trying to do for Beth or the kids, but it often seems to go way off the mark, and ends in disaster. Like the time he went out and bought Beth a chocolate cake. A lovely thought in itself, but he hadn't read the box properly and it was chocolate orange flavour, which Beth detests. That started a whole *'do you even know me?'* argument.

Beth is a whole different person when she's had a few to drink. A five-foot-two, auburn haired firecracker that none of us can keep up with. She drinks to excess, does daft things, then she'll put herself to bed and wake up, as bright as anything, like she'd had an early night. When you have the hangover from hell, she's annoyingly chirpy.

Megan doesn't have any kids, she's younger than the rest of us. She was the apprentice in our office, many moons ago, and we took her under our wing. Now, a decade later, she's one of us. Megan is a bit naïve and she'll often get teased for not knowing basic life facts. Beth convinced her once, while we were meant to be working, that polo neck jumpers are made from polar bear fur. I don't think she's lived that one down to this day. To be fair to Megan, she has, until recently, lived at home with her parents, and been mollycoddled. She's never had to pay bills or cook meals or do anything resembling adult life. At least when we moved out of home, and went to University, we were dumped in at the deep end, and were allowed to make stupid mistakes.

Now Megan lives with her boyfriend who manages everything for her, and not in a good, protective way either. Unfortunately, Megan is *so in love* with this guy she's seeing that she can't see what he's really like. We keep having to rein her in, to stop him from taking over and isolating her completely. There's just something that doesn't sit quite right with him, but she can't see that just yet.

Lizzie is the last of our travelling foursome. She is the no-nonsense, straight talking one. If you want someone's honest opinion, ask Lizzie. If you just want someone to be nice and agree with you, stay well clear. She's the one that tells you your bum looks big in your favourite dress, but there is never any malice.

In fact, that's why I love Lizzie – precisely because she always tells you the truth. When my ex-husband left me I really wanted people to say that everything would be ok. I hoped they'd say that, yes he is probably just having a midlife crisis and would come home once he has realised what a great life he had with us. And they all did, except Lizzie. She told me he was a twat. That he was probably banging someone from his office, that he had never realised what a great life he had, and I was better off without him. Of course, she was absolutely correct and that became apparent quite quickly.

Her kids are with their Dad, Jonathan, this weekend. So are my two. The difference being, I get a break every other weekend, whereas Lizzie and her ex share custody equally. I took the easy option with my divorce and didn't push for joint custody. With such an important job, David couldn't possibly do school runs, school meetings, packed lunches and all the other organisational operation stuff that goes with having kids, so it was just easier to do it all myself. By the way, his job isn't important in the slightest. He's middle management at best. He just likes to think he's big and important and doesn't want the hassle of being a full-time parent.

These girls are my very own dysfunctional family and I can rely on them for anything. They are the people who would dig a patio and help me bury the body.

Back on the draughty platform, we all turn around at the sound of a high-pitched squeal. Sammy's arrived – stilettos, designer sunglasses and all.

"Are you ready Bitches?" She stands there with a bottle of vodka raised to the sky, it's unclear whether she has come straight from another party or she's just wanting to let loose early. Lizzie rolls her eyes while the rest of us swamp her in hugs. This weekend is gonna get messy!

True to form Sammy has rented a swanky pad for us all, close to the city centre. It's got high ceilings and big windows and is already stocked with prosecco, gin, vodka and an array of tinned cocktails. She pours us all a drink while telling us what she has planned.

First off, we are going to some fancy Greek place for meze and frozen daiquiris. Then on to some high-end bars that all the lawyers and bankers regularly frequent. I don't know why she takes us to places like this because we end up having too much to drink and acting like we've been raised by wolves.

The first of the prosecco bottles is popped and we toast our weekend plans, while Megan's phone blings with about eight message alerts, one after another.

"Can you just put that on silent Megan, he doesn't need to know your every move!" Lizzie spits out.

He's probably put a tracker on her phone anyway, but this could go either way. Megan can get very defensive over this bloke, Darren, and his behaviour, but she types a quick message and silences her phone.

"Oh Emma, I have something for you!" Sammy says rifling through her bag. She pulls out some black fabric and chucks it at me so quickly that I almost spill my drink.

"What is it?" I say looking at it from several different angles.

"It's a dress," she says, matter of factly. I give her a head tilt, the confusion on my face obvious. "To go out in tonight!" she says it as if she thinks I'm a bit dense.

"I can dress myself you know Sammy, I brought my own clothes," I throw back, still looking confused.

"Only if you want to look like a librarian." The sarcasm is dripping from her tone.

"That's a bit harsh!" I lift up the dress, trying to work out which way round it goes. Surely there isn't enough fabric in this to fit over everything. "I'll look like a prostitute. Plus, I can't, I haven't shaved my legs." Sammy looks at me deadpan.

"The intended look is MILF or Cougar." I eye roll at her and look round to the others for help. No one wants to step in.

"I've got a razor," pipes up Beth with a wide grin on her face and Sammy looks triumphant.

"Oh yeah and I bought these for you too." She hands me a Harvey Nichols bag and I pull out some black lace fabric. I squint at them trying to figure out what they are.

"You bought me a bra set? Why?"

"Because your tits are your best feature."

"What about my intelligence and sense of humour?" I bite back. She shrugs as if it's nothing. Who even buys their friend lingerie from Harvey Nicks? I look to Lizzie for some help,

"It can't hurt," she says, taking another swig of her drink. Traitor!

"Bitches, the lot of you!" I fluster. Beth laughs and Megan lifts her head up from her phone with a little grin. "Is this some kind of intervention?" I look to each of them as they seem to be all in this together. "I can't wear this, I don't have the body for it, I had two children you know!"

"Yes, a decade and a half ago. You have no excuses now." Sammy seems to be winning.

I did have a mummy body up until the divorce, then stress hit. I stopped eating and I lost a lot of weight. No one noticed though, because I still hid underneath baggy jumpers and leggings.

"And these!" she flings big silver hoop earrings at me.

"I am not 15!" But there's no use arguing, it seems like its four against one, I'll never win. I huff off to my room to get changed.

An hour or so later and everyone is changed and ready to go. I come back into the living area where everyone has congregated, to find they have finished two bottles of prosecco already. I'm trying to pull the dress over my breasts at the same time as pulling it down to cover more of my legs. Its low cut, like really low cut, and very tight. I'm not sure my boobs will stay inside this bra, let alone this dress. It's snug over the top half with capped sleeves, then flares out a little at the waist, stopping just above my knees. This is definitely not a *jeans and a nice top* kind of night.

My hair, which is usually pulled into some non-descript ponytail-come-bun, has been curled so its wavy and shoulder length, courtesy of Beth. I have dark shiny brown curls, somewhere close to my natural tone, if I can even remember what that colour is.

The only thing I have really kept on top of is dying my hair. For one I'm far too young to be sporting grey hair, and for two, I can't stand the thought of seeing different coloured roots. Anyone else would go out to get their nails manicured or hair styled, but I'd be in the bathroom with a boxed colour and some rubber gloves. I once asked Noah to help me wash the dye out, and nearly got drowned by the jets of the shower up my nose. I learnt my lesson that day – don't ask for help from the boys.

We finish off our drinks, which have left us giggly and relaxed, and head for the door. As I'm passing, Sammy pulls my coat out of my hand and throws it on the sofa, giving me *the look*! I'm self-conscious as hell with these unfamiliar clothes, but I figure no one I know is going to see me out in Edinburgh. I'm not going to be bumping into Sandra from the PTA with her judgy comments, so I'll go with it. I straighten up and start to feel like sassy Emma again. Where ever did *she* even go?

Chapter Three

The night is progressing very well. Luckily we've had some food to soak up all the alcohol. Unluckily we have just added more and more alcohol on top. We get to the door of our third bar of the night, the cocktails have been flowing so far and they have warmed us up. Everyone is relaxed and having a great time.

Beth has only called Steve twice in the last hour, which is some feat. Megan isn't looking at her phone but laughing to the point of snorting at something Lizzie just said. I've stopped pulling the dress up and down and I've linked arms with Sammy. She towers over me in her stilettos. But the way she can walk in them, you'd think they were trainers.

We can hear how busy this bar is without even opening the doors. We are greeted by bouncers who are not like the ones you'd get at home. They are toned like they have made no effort, and gorgeous as hell. Beth is already giving them the eye. They open the door and the bar is big but pretty full. Music is pumping but the noise levels come from the sheer amount of people in the place. It's nothing like the Dog and Swan back home. It smells different for a start. You can't smell stale alcohol or the gents' toilets. It looks high-end and sleek but so do the people inside.

Sammy talks to the person at the door and we all try to peer further inside to check out what's going on. We definitely wouldn't get in without Sammy's connections and status. I imagine this place is packed with professionals.

We are directed past the bar, which looks colourful with hundreds of different bottles and styles of glasses, over to a high table with stools around it. I very ungracefully clamber up to perch on a stool. I'm only five-foot-four, so everything is a bit of a hike. I don't like to stand around fashionably like most people. I like the comfort of sitting. Plus it means I can see more from this higher stance. Drinks menus are put on the table by the ridiculously beautiful waitress. It's more like a catalogue than a menu, but I don't need one. I'm having my favourite, French Martini. The others stand around and discuss options before the waitress saunters over to take the order.

"Look what's over there," Lizzie says, nodding her head sideways toward a group of men. "I can smell the testosterone from here." She scrunches her nose. Lizzie doesn't hate men, but is very much a feminist. Men can see it a mile off, but when alcohol is a-plenty, they seem to flock to her because she is a challenge. Some don't even get to open their mouths before they get a curt *Fuck off!*.

These men are different. They scream money and masculinity. They are all buttoned up shirts, rolled up sleeves and expensive watches. We can smell their mix of cologne – they smell good enough to eat.

"You need to look at their shoes," says Beth. "You can always tell the calibre of men by their shoes."

"To be fair, everyone in this place is dripping with money, so I don't think we can use that as a differential here," Lizzie states. She's right though, normally there would be a few different types of men we can spot. There's the rich, the sports lads, stag dos, they all have their own telltale look. But this place is different. It seems every group of people can be classed as rich-professional. The group of men in question look over and exchange commentary with each other, just like we have. There is movement from the group, one of them taking the initiative to engage with us.

"Well hello there, lovely ladies! Can I buy you some drinks?" The spokesman is well turned out, but he has a bit of an Eton Boy look of him, matched with his posh accent.

"Nope!" Lizzie bites back within a second, giving the P a pop sound. The rest of us laugh out loud, knowing he's been well and truly put in his place. His face drops for a moment but then he smiles and attempts to try again. Lizzie puts her hand up in a stop sign and he stands statue still. It's obvious that he isn't used to being rejected like this, maybe he thought we would just giggle and fawn all over him and his friends, deluded! Another man steps round in front of him to face the wrath of women who couldn't give a shit.

"Sorry about him, he doesn't get out much." He nods to his friend. This new man is gorgeous, piercing blue eyes and a physique as if he is the blue print for all gorgeous men. He puts his hand on his chest. "I'm Ben and it would be amazing if you beautiful ladies would join us for a drink." His sultry smooth Edinburgh accent, along with his winning smile, wins the crowd. He sounds genuine and nice. Lizzie nods, giving him the green light to continue. "These are my friends," he starts to point them out. "Sean, Joel and that dickhead is Piers." They all give us a little wave, Piers very sheepish after being shot down by Lizzie.

"You're gorgeous... I mean I'm Beth!" Beth's hand goes straight to her mouth, the drink loosening her lips and she is just saying whatever is in her head. He smiles a warm smile. The other girls take turns to introduce themselves and Ben steps closer to me. He looks from my feet all the way up and meets my eyes, it's as if there was no one else around. The air crackles with electricity. It takes me a few moments to realise he's waiting for my name.

"Oh yes, I'm Emma," I blurt out. Attractive men make me nervous. I end up tongue tied and sounding like a complete idiot, so I generally keep quiet.

"Well it's lovely to meet you Emma." He's not taken his eyes off me. "Can I get everyone a drink?" He says this to everyone, but seems to be directing the question straight to me.

"Erm," I respond. He's still looking at me and everyone seems to just be watching the exchange. Lizzie coughs and we are pulled out of the trance. "Erm yeah, I'll have a French Martini," I manage, eventually. Lizzie rolls her eyes.

"Thanks!" Sammy takes over. "I'll have a Pornstar Martini, Lizzie will have a Cuba Libra, Megan and Beth will have margaritas, but Beth better have a lemonade chaser too cos she's a lightweight. Want any help?"

"No, I'm good," he replies. He eventually breaks the eye contact and calls over a waitress and reels off our order. We all move about to accommodate the larger group around the table, and everyone starts chatting. Ben moves back round to stand in front of me, drinking me in without saying a word. The air around us buzzes and I feel a shiver down my back.

"I haven't seen you around, do you come here often?" He puts his head in his hands, embarrassed. "Sorry, that was terrible! I mean, well, I don't know. Argh this isn't as smooth as I hoped."

I laugh, it's quite a change from it being me who is tongue tied. It gives me a bit of confidence, knowing that someone so gorgeous, and who probably chats up women a lot, can feel it too.

"No, I don't come here often. We are visiting Sammy on our girls' weekend. Mums on tour and all that." Now it's time for me to cringe. I don't know why I can't just pretend to be someone with no worries or ties, a single, up for anything type.

Ben raises his eyebrows. "Well, you know what they say! What goes on tour, stays on tour?"

"Ha yes! First rule of fight club and all that..." I shake my head realising I'm talking utter rubbish. My cringe is saved by the waitress coming back and dishing out the drinks.

"So tell me a bit about yourself. Your job maybe?"

I wince at the question. "Look, I'm really not that interesting. I have a boring job and an even more boring life, so these *getting to know you* questions will put you right off!"

"Okay then." He thinks for a moment. "Let's do this another way. Quick fire questions, first answer that comes into your head. These are quite sophisticated questions though." He gives me a wink. "Ready?"

"Ready!"

"Marmite. Yes or no?"

"Eww no!"

"Tea or coffee?"

"Tea mainly, except on a morning."

"So when do you add the milk, first or last?"

"That really depends on how you make it. If it's from a tea pot, the milk goes in first. If it's a teabag in a cup, then last." He raises his eyebrows at me. "Unless you take sugar, then it's last on both counts."

"You've thought about this haven't you?"

"Yes I'm a self-confessed overthinker."

He laughs. "If you could only eat one meal for the rest of your life, what would it be?"

"Pizza!"

"Good Choice. Supplementary question.... Does pineapple belong on Pizza."

"Hell yeah."

"Heathen!" He pulls an disgusted face. "Favourite biscuit?"

"Ooh that's a tough one. Maybe one of those chocolate covered cookies, or a bourbon."

"Nice."

"Chocolate or sex?"

"Chocolate!"

"You haven't been sleeping with the right man then."

"You're right there. Okay, my turn." I grin up at him and he readies himself, cracking his knuckles. "How many women have you slept with?"

His face falls. "Oh that's not fair!"

"I know but your face was a picture!" I laugh at him. "Okay for real now, ready?"

"Ready!"

"Bacon butty or smashed avocado on toast?"

"Bacon butty hands down."

"Red or brown sauce?"

"Depends what it is but mainly brown."

"Sports car or people SUV?"

"Sports car!"

"Date night or lads' night?"

"Well I'm currently on a lads' night, but if I was with you it would be date night." I roll my eyes at him and he gives me a cheeky smile.

"Is Die Hard a Christmas film?"

"Yes!"

"Wrong! Okay last one. Rate my friends in order. The first being the most fanciable."

"That's also not fair!" He shifts uncomfortably.

"I won't tell them. We can't move on until you answer."

Eventually he realises he isn't going to win. "You first, obviously."

"Is it obvious?"

"Yes!" He gives me a funny look. "Then Sammy, then the dark haired one..."

"Megan?"

"Yes. Then the little feisty one."

"Beth!"

"Yes, then Lizzie. Lizzie is only last because I'm a bit scared of her."

"Everyone is!"

We chat a bit more about general things and the conversation is easy and natural. He is charming but not sleezy and down to earth, not what I expected from a bar like this.

We must have been chatting for an hour, but it feels like minutes. I take another sip of my cocktail, which is going down very well. I also learn that the boys all work together in one form or another and tonight they are out for their monthly guys' night on the town.

Ben leans into me again to start speaking, the noise is a good excuse to get up close. He starts to say something and is jostled forward as someone pushes past him, tipping the rest of my drink down my front. I can feel the cold, sticky liquid going down my cleavage and soaking through the dress. Ben's shocked face is focused on my chest, making me very aware of the lack of fabric covering it. He grabs a napkin and goes to soak up the mess but thinks better of it.

"I'm so sorry!" He looks mortified. I take the napkin and wipe myself down as he fusses around.

"It's okay, not your fault, I'm fine really." I excuse myself to go to the ladies, slip off the stool and brush past his hard body. I shudder at the connection. He is so gorgeous. His body, I can tell even through his clothes, is sculptured. His face is angular with a jaw full of stubble, and his brown hair, obviously cut recently but not styled, looks like he has just put his hands through it. But he's too gorgeous for me and so young, probably late twenties. But it's nice to get a bit of attention.

I get into the toilets, but they look more like a boutique than a convenience. There are mirrors all along the walls that look like something from a fairy-tale scene and the rest of the place is all marble and chrome. As I try to get the sticky mess from out of my bra with a towel, I look in the mirror, which seems to have some kind of filter on. Or was it the amount I have drunk? I wonder what it would be like to be with a man like Ben. I shake my head, coming to my senses, fix my lipstick, put my fingers through my hair and pull on the door out into the corridor. I turn to head back to our table, but he's there, leaning back, knee bent, foot on the wall. Our eyes meet and a smile curls the side of his mouth as he pushes off the wall towards me.

"Hi!" he says looking right at me, like he can see into my soul.

"Hi yourself!" I reply, sounding way more confident than I actually feel.

"Did you get cleaned up okay." He looks apologetic.

"I think I'll be smelling of cocktails for the rest of the night," I say with a shrug. He looks at me with those piercing eyes and my mind goes blank.

"I thought we could..." he pauses, "...talk maybe, away from the others."

"Okay" I draw out with a puzzled look.

"Or maybe I could just kiss you like I actually wanted!" He comes closer, backing me up against the wall with a subtle movement. I can feel his hard body press against me and he moves closer. He leans in with his hands placed either side of my face, caging me in. As he gets close, my pulse increases and a flush goes up my neck. I'm on unfamiliar ground here, this man, who smells amazing and exudes masculinity, is so close I can feel his body heating up.

The conflicting emotions, the fight or flight of this situation. I want him to kiss me so much it hurts, but why is he wanting me?

My pulse is through the roof. This kind of thing never happens to me. Sammy yes, but not me! He leans in further, his face reaching mine. I can smell his delicious cologne mixed with strong spiced alcohol.

"Okay," I say again. I seem to have lost all words and any coherent thoughts. His lips meet mine gently, almost as if I'm imagining it, and he pulls away slightly. He moves forward again and plants another, more firmly this time. As he pulls away again, my breath hitches. Can he see that I'm in totally out of my depth here? He looks at me again. The few seconds feel like a lifetime, then he tilts his head, opens his lips and kisses me again. This time I know he's after more. His tongue glides across my teeth and I open up to him, his tongue tickling mine. The kiss turns frantic. I don't even remember the last time anyone kissed me on the mouth, let alone like they wanted to consume me. David never really kissed me once the children were born, not even with sex. I had forgotten how amazing it felt and I don't want to let go.

His hand drops to the outside of my thigh and goes slowly higher. I don't know how they got there but I have my hand behind his neck and I'm pulling at his hair, the other is round his waist, pulling him close. His fingertips slide under the elastic of my pants and squeeze my bum. I pull away from his mouth taking in a large gulp of air, like I have been given the kiss of life. He leans back to give me room. "You okay?" he says, looking at me like I'm about to bolt. And to be fair, I am.

"We best get back. They'll wonder where we are and send out a search party."

He moves back again giving me enough room to escape and he follows me to the table, leaving enough of a gap that no one thinks we were together.

As I clamber onto the stool, I feel his strong arm around me helping me up. He looks at me and smiles, but his eyes are saying something different, questioning my reluctance.

The girls are all laughing and joking with the group but I'm unusually quiet. The conversation flows around us and no one else notices the tension. He stands to the side of me draping, his arm across the back of my stool, then he moves closer to whisper in my ear. "Did you not enjoy that? Because I REALLY enjoyed that kiss!"

We look at each other, both waiting for the other to speak. "I can't!" I say, breaking his gaze. His face flashes with an expression that I can't quite read. I'm not sure why I have rejected something that was so nice. Ok I absolutely do! Because it's just not me. I can't change who I am, not even for one night of anonymity. I've never been someone who can have a one-night stand, not even at university. Sammy, on the other hand, I have found in many a compromising position with people she'd met a few hours before. I, though, dated guys until they got bored of me or I just didn't bother.

"Okay," he says with a look that says he's still trying to work me out.

I manoeuvre myself back into the group's conversation. I hadn't realised how animated they had all got with each other until now. They're all involved in some way. Beth is draped over a scared looking Joel. Megan is showing Sean something on her phone and they both laugh. Lizzie and Sammy are taking it in turns to arm wrestle with Piers. Bunch of maniacs the lot of them. Lizzie gives me a quizzical look, like she can't work out what I'm thinking, then announces to the group, "let's go to a club!" Everyone except me cheers.

"Aren't we too old to go clubbing?" She gives me a *whatever* look, stands up, pulls me off the stool and marches me out of the bar, the rest following with no hesitation.

Chapter Four

Oh god... Now I'm being brought back to reality, waking up with one eye glued shut, the other letting in the sharp beam of light from the crack in the blinds.

At least I know I'm still alive. I must be because my head is pounding, and my mouth feels like I haven't had a drink in months, yet I have a trail of dried-up drool at the corner of it. What the hell happened last night?

You know in films where they do a montage of snippets of scenes in a club, strobe lights, pounding music and all that. Well that's my recollection of the nightclub. I don't really remember getting there or getting inside. I remember shots that burnt on the way down. I remember getting pulled on the dancefloor with the girls. I remember laughing *a lot*. I remember Beth dancing on a podium. I remember dancing with hands in the air, jumping up and down in a sea of sweaty bodies. I remember Ben. Oh god, Ben. I remember him being so close to me, holding my hips while we danced together. I remember unbuttoning his shirt in the middle of the dancefloor, but after that, not much.

Then I remember just us girls, out in the street walking, singing, arm in arm. I cringe as I remember taking Megan's phone off her, and me, Sammy and Lizzie talking to her boyfriend and not being particularly pleasant. Oops. I remember a food van of some description, but I don't remember eating anything. Then us all falling through the door of the apartment, leaving a trail of shoes and bags. Beth went straight and put herself to bed, as she always does. Sammy faceplanted the sofa. Megan was face down on the floor. Lizzie just pottered around as if it was any other night.

I slowly sit up, realising I only managed to put my pyjama top on. I don't know where my clutch bag is, or my phone for that matter. There's movement out in the living area, so I peel myself off the bed, pull on my pyjama bottoms and head out.

Beth is standing in the kitchen making coffee, looking as fresh as a daisy, showered, clothed and wearing perfect makeup.

"How the hell do you look like that this morning?" I ask her through squinted eyes. She just laughs and hands me a coffee. Typical Beth!

"Your phone was blowing up first thing this morning but died before I could see who it was. I plugged it in for you." She nods over to the phone plugged into the charger on the kitchen worktop. Picking it up I power it on. As soon as its awake it starts binging with notifications and I turn it to silent. My head can't deal with that much noise this morning.

Before I can see who has been trying to get hold of me, the screen pops up with an incoming call. The screen display says David. I show the screen to Beth with a frown.

"What does knobhead want at this time in the morning? He knows full well you're away," she asks. I shrug and answer the call.

"What time are you getting back?" No pleasantries.

"Well, good morning David!" I say sarcastically. He doesn't give any acknowledgement of his lack of formalities.

"I need to drop the boys back early. I've had something important come up."

"David, I'm in Edinburgh. I can't just drop everything." I pinch the top of my nose with my thumb and finger, trying to stop the pounding and growing frustration. "My train gets in around two, so I'll be back about half past," I finish.

"Well that doesn't suit me today," he says abruptly.

"Tough shit!" I bite back. I have even surprised myself with that statement. But I don't have the patience today after last night's alcohol consumption and lack of sleep. I hang up before he can say any more. I can't be bothered with a fight this early on. Beth is looking at me with a smirk on her face. "WHAT?" I snap.

"Absolutely nothing." She grins, holding her hands up in a surrender sign. I chuck my phone back on the side, not ready to face any more and saunter back to my room, trying not to make any sudden movements.

One by one all the girls gather back in the living area, in various states of hung over, searching for missing items. I have showered, dressed and am feeling a little bit more human. Beth and Megan are on one of the two chesterfield-type leather sofas with hands huddled around their coffee mugs. Lizzie and Sammy are in the kitchen, picking at various bits of food.

The reconstruction of the previous night has already started without me. Lizzie, as always, remembers every moment. She often doesn't share all she has seen. I'm wondering whether that's to keep it for ammunition for another time or that she's really not that bothered. Megan generally doesn't remember anything at all.

"You went AWOL for a bit last night Em, what happened?" Sammy asks.

"I have absolutely no idea." I'm not sure I would even tell them if I remembered. But she looks at me with squinted eyes. "No, I really have no clue."

"Might it have anything to do with that gorgeous man you had your hands all over?"

I shrug and pick up my now fully charged phone, to look at the notifications, I just presumed it was David that had been ringing and I didn't want to engage. But when I bring up the missed call list none are from him.

I look at the contact name and have no idea who it is. I look back at the screen with squinted eyes, as if that's going to make any difference. Who could 'Love of Your Life' be? I click into the contact and see Ben's photo. I have a flash back to him with my phone, taking selfies of himself and the two of us. He must have used one of those for this contact. I open my gallery and there's all the evidence of the night before and I cringe a little, realising that I had let my guard down. I open my messages and he's sent all of the images to his phone.

My phone lights up displaying his face and I drop it like its stung me. Should I answer it? What would I say? What if I did something stupid last night? I look up and the rest of the group have stopped what they were doing and are staring at me.

"Is that knobhead again?" Beth asks.

"Nope. It's ... erm... Ben!"

"Answer it then!" she says. I'm totally flustered with indecision, but Sammy picks up the phone and presses accept before passing it back to me. I'm still looking at it in my hand when I hear the velvet Scottish accent.

"Emma?" I'm gonna have to speak now, instead of hanging up.

"Erm yes... Hi!"

"Thank god, I was worried. You all just left without a word. I was checking you were all okay."

"Yes, we're fine. Not quite sure how we got home, but we are all here and.... Hungover!" I say followed by silence.

"Good, I had pictured all kinds of things. We were talking about greasy food one minute and the next thing you were gone." I look up and the girls are still staring at me. I give them a little shrug. "There's another thing," he says. "I have your bank card."

"How have you got that?" Something else I don't remember.

"Well I gave you my business card and you thought giving me your bank card was a fair exchange." He must think I'm an absolute idiot. He gives a little laugh then continues. "I thought I could meet you before you get your train home." Oh god! I'm going to have to see him again looking like crap, feeling like crap, wondering what kind of tit I made of myself last night. Well at least he will realise that I'm not the catch he might think in my normal *librarian* clothes, greasy hair and no make-up. "We could meet up for breakfast or something?" he says with a note of hope in his voice.

"Breakfast?" The girls nod, mouthing yesses across the board. "Erm... we've already had breakfast." The girls are now jumping up and down gesticulating to me. The five of us are having a silent but very animated back and forth, with them trying to get me to agree, while Ben waits patiently. "Maybe you could just meet me at the station to drop it off?" Each of the girl's expressions is a different way to tell me I've done the wrong thing and I shrug giving them wide eyes, which tells them to mind their own business.

"Okay..." he says and I think he sounds disappointed but it could just be wishful thinking. "When's your train?"

"12.30, so I'll see you outside at about ten past." I've given no time for any kind of analysis of the previous night or cosy catch up.

"Right! Entrance on Market Street?"

"Yep. See you then. Bye!" I hang up before he can answer, and the girls just stare at me.

"What the actual fuck was that?" Sammy starts.

"What?" I act like I have no idea what she is talking about.

"Erm, let's see! So you hook up with a totally gorgeous man, who actually seems like a great bloke, who you seemed really into and who seemed REALLY into you, who wants to see you again, and you say no!"

"And your point is?"

"Her point is..." Lizzie interjects, "What's stopping you?"

"We have to get back home!" I make the point.

"Not for a few hours." She states. "Why will you never choose something for yourself?"

"And what would it actually achieve though, a happily ever after? I've got too much going on at the minute. We even live in different countries." Sammy rolls her eyes. But I want this conversation shut down so I try to change the subject. "Can we talk about Beth's podium dancing instead?"

"Beth did what?" Megan asks the group, confirming the fact that she never remembers anything about our nights out.

"I don't know why you look so shocked, Megan." Lizzie has everyone's attention now. "You were getting quite cosy with that tall one. What's his name?"

"Huh!" Megan's face tells us she has no clue. Then realisation hits. "Oh that was Sean. He was cute, we watched cat videos on his phone."

"Bloody likely story."

I put my head down and start to potter, so the subject of my little fling can't be reignited.

Sammy hands me a bacon roll and looks at me straight in the eye. "You okay?"

"Yeah, I'm fine." I touch my head as I search for some painkillers. "Well mainly!"

"What is the real reason why you don't want to get together with this Ben?"

"That was the real reason."

She gives me a look and I'm guilted into delving deeper. "He's gonna see me without his beer goggles and wonder what the hell he was thinking. And who wants someone with this much baggage hanging around?"

"Maybe, you should let go of some of that baggage." She gives me a little grin, "like by pushing it off a cliff." I laugh but I'm never going to get away from David and he's never going to become a more reasonable person.

The girls are comparing the bumps and bruises we have collected throughout the night, trying to piece it all together.

"The side of my legs seems to be bruised. How the hell did i get them?" I rub my hands up and down the outsides of my thighs with a pained expression.

"Maybe that's were Ben was grabbing you?" I give Beth a *that's not funny* look.

"Are you sure you didn't have sex with him?"

"I'm not that kind of girl!" I say with a look of disgust, but at the same time my brain is frantically searching for memories that I may well have done something stupid while under the influence.

"I know how you can tell." Pipes up Sammy, "Just do a big cough." She bursts our laughing. "Then you'll know, unless he's really small."

"He's not." I say without missing a beat and I surprise myself. All the girls at look at me and my face flushes. "Come to think if it, I would definitely know if I had, for at least a few days." They are all gawping at me now and I need to change the subject.

"Go Emma."

"Oh hang on. I remember." Thank god for Lizzie, "I gave you a piggyback on the way home and you kept complaining I was pinching."

Phew! "So you admit now that you were pinching?"

"Absolutely not!"

Chapter Five

I stand on the street outside the station, waiting for him. The girls are inside, knowing that watching the scene between us unfold isn't going to happen, I've made that very clear. I hear his car before I see it come round the corner. He is driving a low, black obnoxious sports car, a Lamborghini or something equally as flashy. He pulls up next to me and gets out, closes the door and leans himself casually on the car.

I give him the once over and he's even more spectacular than I remember. His hair is roughly curled on the top like he doesn't care. He's casually dressed in a grey t-shirt that fits around his hard, sculptured body, dark jeans and new looking trainers. He's doesn't look like he was out last night.

I gave myself a pep talk before he arrived, but looking at him, that's gone straight out of the window. I side eye at his car, raised eyebrows.

"Do you like it?" he nods to the car.

"It's a bit flashy!" I say, unimpressed.

He laughs, "Maybe I'm a bit flashy."

Chapter Six

Ben

There's a knock on my office door, I look up from my laptop to see Sean coming in. He's not really interrupting because I've not been particularly productive this week. I can't get my mind off a certain dark-haired woman. Sean gives me a quizzical look.

"What's up boss?" I shrug. "Have you phoned her yet?" How does he know that my mind is on her and not on this latest acquisition?

"No!" I snap. Don't get me wrong, I've thought about it, I've even pulled her contact up on my phone, but I just haven't pressed call.

"What's stopping you? She said you could call her."

"No, she said *sure*. Which is what people say when they don't want to do something but don't want to argue."

"Well, you're gonna have to do something because you've been a pain in the arse all week." Sean's right, I have been a complete dick. I can't think straight, all I can think about is Emma. There's just something about her. She makes me feel something that I haven't felt with other women and I can't put my finger on it.

I'm no Casanova, well not anymore. I'm usually a bit indifferent about the women I hook up with. I mean, when I'm with them I'm the perfect, attentive boyfriend type. But once I have left their bedroom, I don't think about them again until the next time I get a booty call. I don't know their favourite things or what they like to do when I don't see them. I don't check in on them so see *how they are feeling*, and if that makes me a shit, then so be it. It's never really bothered me before. I don't have the time to play games or happy families.

But Emma is something else. Of course she is gorgeous and she doesn't even realise it. And not to forget she is sexy as hell. The number of times I have jerked off in the shower at the thought of those plump lips around my dick is ridiculous. I think about how amazing she'd feel around me, squeezing and pulsing when she comes. But it's not just that. She's also funny, sweet, quirky. And she looks out for everyone around her.

I loved spending time with her. She's easy to be around, like she isn't playing games. In fact she doesn't even seem to know there is a game. On Saturday night, it was like no one else was around, she had my undivided attention and then she just disappeared when my back was turned. I must have known she was a flight risk because I got her to give me her phone so I could get her number. I couldn't guarantee that giving her my business card would have the right effect. At least she gave me a reason to see her before she left to go home on Sunday. When I saw her, I just wanted to scoop her up, put her in my car and drive off into the sunset. I have officially lost the plot.

And then there's this week, all I can think is 'I wonder what Emma's doing now? I wonder if she has thought about phoning me. I wonder if she has remembered the times we were pressed up against each other. I wonder if she has thought about me and touched herself'. I really need to stop this and sort my head out, it's just not like me.

"Well if she is a nonstarter, just fuck her out of your system with one of your usual girls," Sean says, matter of fact.

"It's complicated!"

"What's so complicated?" he asks. "You don't usually have to think twice about a hook up. Call her, meet up, shag her, forget her! What's complicated about that?" Usually I would agree, and that's my normal MO, but this time it's different.

"It's not that easy. She's affected me and I can't just fuck her out of my system. I can't explain!" I turn back to my screen. What am I going to do? I'm going to have to call her or I think I'll lose my mind.

"Is it because she's turned you down? Now it's a challenge?"

"No! I'm not a fucking predator. If I genuinely thought that she didn't like me and didn't want it to go any further, I'd back the fuck off. But I don't think that's the case. It's like she's not allowing herself to want me or for anything to happen."

"So she's got baggage? You hate complicated chicks! How much baggage are we talking?"

"An ex-husband, two teenage boys and self-esteem that's in the gutter!"

"Wow, that's a lot of complicated. I'd run a mile!" He wouldn't, he's a nicer guy than me. Well, he is when he actually opens up that heart of stone. But he also knows me too well.

"I know and usually I would run for the fucking hills. But she's... I don't know... different!" I sigh. I really don't know what I'm doing. I'm flip flopping between wanting to scoop her up, to be the one who saves her, and just sacking it off and leaving it as just another good night out. I need to call her! But I'm going to have to get my shit together before I do. Because every time I talk to her I'm back to being a bumbling teenage boy, not able to get my words out.

Sean pulls me out of my thoughts. "Well you better get your mind back on the job. We have a meeting with Joel in ten minutes to see if we can free up some equity for the next stage of this riverside build."

He's right, I have to stop daydreaming about her because my decision-making is getting compromised. I think I'll have to burn off some of this nervous energy in the gym before I attempt to make contact. My phone bleeps with an incoming message and I check the screen hoping it will be from her. And of course it isn't.

Ami: Hi stud! Still on for dinner tonight?

Ben: Yes, meet at the restaurant at 7

Ami: xxx

At least I'll have Ami to distract me tonight. With that, I gather my things and follow Sean out of the door.

Chapter Seven

Emma

God, it has been a long week. It's Friday evening and, as ever, the only plans I have are with a glass of wine and a boxset of whatever it is this week. The boys are with me this weekend, but I won't see them. They'll break away from their gaming and YouTube long enough to get their dinner and take it back up to their rooms, or to ask for money to get something, and that will be it.

The next few days will be no better, I'll need to do the food shop and the school uniform wash. I really need to get out of this rut. I'm not living my life, I'm just existing. It's no better when the boys are with their dad. You'd think I'd make an effort to go somewhere and do something, but other than a meet up with the girls, its much of the same. But where do I start getting my life back on track?

I know I complained at the time about Sammy's intervention with my wardrobe, but actually I kind of liked it. The clothes made me feel exciting, sexy and even just seen. I wasn't that nearly forty-year-old mum, I was Emma. Fun Emma!

Most people get divorced and have some kind of rebirth, but not me. It was like everything had changed, yet nothing at all. I grab my phone and open the group chat.

Me: SOS!!!

Beth: What's happened?

Me: I need some wardrobe help.

Lizzie: Yes, indeed you do!

Megan: TBF Em, you do look like something the 2000s has left behind.

Me: Cheers for that, not helpful.

Beth: Well what do you want to do?

Me: Well I can't afford a whole new wardrobe so I need help going through what I already have.

Lizzie: ...erm...

Beth: *gasps*

Megan: Do you have anything that's actually salvageable?

Well that's a bit harsh. I know I've been mainly wearing functional clothing recently, but still!

Me: Bitches! That's really not helpful.

Lizzie: So you've heard from Ben then!

Me: No. What makes you say that?

Lizzie: I thought that might have been the catalyst for this change.

Me: No, it's not. But Saturday made me feel different. The clothes I mean. Not the man. I don't need a bloke to make me want more from my life.

Lizzie: Good for you! About bloody time!

Beth: I'm on my way round.

Megan: Me too! I'll bring wine.

Lizzie: I really can't be arsed, and it's not my field of expertise.

Me: Okay, see you soon, and be kind... I'm actually glad you're not coming Liz!!!!!

I put my phone down, but as if there's a psychic intervention, my phone starts to ring. His photo flashes on the screen. Should I answer? I said he could call, but I just don't really see the point if it's never going to happen. I answer anyway, because I hate being rude. And I really want to hear his gorgeous voice again.

"Emma?" Oh my god, he sounds delicious. I remember putting my hands all over him that night. I have another flash back of kissing him in the club, deep and desperate. I shake my head trying to get my head together.

"Hi... I really should change your contact name in my phone. People will start to talk!"

"Why change it when it's true? I'm not changing my contact for you." He has a light laughter to his voice that seems to calm my nerves.

"What is it?" He laughs and there a ping on my phone. When I look, he's sent me a picture. I open it up and it's a screen shot with my photo on. I've never seen the picture before, but it's actually quite flattering. It's a side view of me sipping a cocktail through a straw. He obviously took it on the sly when we were out. The contact name is 'My Princess'.

"Well, I'm a bit too old to be a princess. Maybe a Dowager Duchess!" I state. "Did you just call for a chat? Because I'm a bit busy." A lie. I've got all the time in the world.

"No... well yes, I wanted to hear your voice again, but I also called to see if we could meet up."

"I don't see how that will be possible. It's not like you live round the corner." I hear him sigh down the phone, so I continue with the excuses. "We live completely different lives. Geographically we are hundreds of miles away, and I have... stuff going on."

"Yes, I know about the STUFF. You keep mentioning it. But you can't ignore the fact that there was something between us last weekend." At least he felt it too. "And I know you'll say that you had a few to drink and it is out of character for you and it wouldn't work between us. Because you've mentioned that a few times too." There's another pause as if he's pulling back his frustration. "But what if it did? What if we were made for each other?" He pauses but I know he hasn't finished. "I can't stop thinking about you, Emma. I've done absolutely no work this week. So even for the sake of me not going bankrupt AND putting Sean and Joel out of a job, I think we need to try at least, see what happens."

There's another big pause, I just don't know what to say to him. Talking was easy when we were out, but I just don't know what to say. I can't tell him I've been thinking about him too, that I keep daydreaming about peeling off all his clothes. Maybe he's right and we do have to do something.

"What did you have in mind?" I say eventually. I can hear a relieved sigh as if he had been holding his breath this whole time.

"Well I could come down when the kids are next with their dad. Take you out for dinner. If you decide you don't like me after that, we'll just leave it." He knows full well that I do like him.

"So you're just going to drive all the way down here for dinner, then drive all the way back after?" I need to know his intentions. Does he expect to stay here for the night, that we'll have sex? Is that why he's coming? For just a quick hook up?

"No I'll drive all the way down and stay some place close. If you don't want to see me after that I'll drive back. But if you do and you will, we can arrange to meet up again." He's definitely thought about this. I can't really fault the plan.

"Okay!" I say.

"You mean okay I can take you to dinner?" There is a hint of surprise in his voice, maybe I gave in too quickly.

"Yes! You can take me to dinner! The boys are with their dad next weekend. Do you want to come down on the Friday or Saturday maybe?"

"Definitely Friday. I'll wrap up work early and head down. Is there anywhere you would like to go?

"You choose, but don't bring the flashy car. The neighbours will talk." He laughs again. The doorbell rings, signalling the arrival of the girls. "There's someone at the door, I've got to go." I say quickly, before I change my mind.

"Okay, see you Friday. Bye!" I put the phone down and go for the door with a hundred panicked, overthinking thoughts running through my head.

Chapter Eight

The week has gone by in a whirlwind. The girls came over on Friday night and absolutely destroyed my wardrobe. I was nearly in tears and had to drown my sorrows in a few bottles of wine. Even my underwear got thrown out. They said they couldn't save anything but I managed to fish some of my favourite things out of the bin. That triggered the need for a shopping trip for some new work and evening wear. As if I need 'evening wear' but after I told the girls about the dinner with Ben, they absolutely insisted on it.

I absolutely hate clothes shopping. The time it takes to actually find something you might like, then having to try it on and it looking completely different on you than it did on the mannequin. But it was nice to be with the girls and also to feel like I actually have some semblance of a figure. We found things in the sale so my credit card didn't get that much of a thrashing, but thinking about the change in my appearance had me in a bit of a panic. I don't know what it was, maybe just that I could feel a change coming and I'd been holding onto the past like some kind of security blanket.

I tried out my new work look this week, with a tight black pencil skirt matched with floaty cream blouse that tied at the neck with a ruffle. I decided that although I would wear heels, I'd keep my ballet pumps in my bag just in case. Let's not run before we can walk, metaphorically and literally.

It is safe to say I am no longer invisible in the office. Maureen from finance asked if it was really me with a screwed-up face like she'd swallowed a wasp. Other people just kept watching me as if they couldn't believe what I looked like. The drivers actually lifted their faces out of their newspapers this morning. I'm not sure whether I like the new attention or not. Being anonymous is great, especially in such an outdated office environment.

Beth keeps giving me the thumbs up over her monitor for encouragement, but I think it just makes me feel more out of place. There has been many mutterings around the office about a mid-life crisis and a new love interest. And as if he knew how to feed the gossip factory perfectly, Ben sent 12 white roses to my office yesterday afternoon, with a card that said, 'I can't wait the see you, B x'. Of course, everyone that came in and thought it was their right to read the card. I ended up putting the card in my purse. And if I could have hidden the flowers under my desk I would have, but with all the years of junk under it, there just wasn't enough space.

I came home to another delivery, this time from Sammy. When I unwrapped the box I found a pair of patent leather heels with a bow on the back of each. They are gorgeous and must have cost a small fortune. I'm not sure how Sammy thinks I'm gonna stay upright in them though.

It's six o'clock on Friday, and I've had a few messages from Ben through the week. His last was to say he had set off and he wasn't in the flashy car. I keep looking at my watch. David should have picked the boys up half an hour ago but there has been no sign and no message.

Maybe he has spoken to the boys, so I shout up the stairs. Three times I shout for Josh, each time sounding more and more deranged. I pick up my phone and ring him, but from the very few words I get out of him, David hasn't been in touch.

I decide to bite the bullet and ring him myself. I try to have as little contact with him as possible, because he always ends up making me feel inferior. He has a way of making me feel shit about myself in only a few words.

"Hiya David, when are you getting here to pick the boys up?" I say, trying to keep the irritation out of my voice.

"Something has come up, I can't get them tonight, I might be able to get them tomorrow."

"What the fuck David? This is getting ridiculous. Do you think you could have given me more notice? I have plans," I bite back. I have been a bag of nerves at the thought of seeing Ben and I can't deal with this complication. But I also can't tell David that he has ruined my date.

"Well I can't help it if something comes up. I'm sure you can rearrange your night of binge watching TV to another night." I see red!

"So this *something* is more important than spending time with your children?"

"Well it helps clothe and feed our children, so it is pretty important, yes!" There's the venom that he uses to make me feel like I'm being unreasonable and ungrateful. But it doesn't have the same effect it usually does. Instead of shying away from a fight, this time I'm absolutely fuming.

"For fuck's sake David..."

I hang up and immediately dial Ben. "Ben!" I can't get the fury out of my voice and I know that my anger and frustration are now going to be aimed at the wrong person.

"Hiya Princess! I'm not far from you now." He hasn't noticed that I'm raging.

"I have to cancel our date!" I rip the band aid off.

"What the fuck Emma?"

"I'm sorry. The boys' dad isn't coming to collect them, so I can't go." I hear him sigh, trying to control his temper.

"Emma!" His voice low and there's a pause while he thinks of the correct words. "I'm driving, and I think we better have this conversation when I've stopped. I'm nearly at my hotel so I'll call you when I'm there." He hangs up before I can answer.

I pace around the kitchen, getting more and more worked up. I'm half ready for the night, I just have to put on my dress and shoes. I didn't want David to see me and give him an excuse to question what I was doing and where I was going. I'm annoyed with myself as well as him. I've let him get away with constantly changing plans, because I didn't have anything better to do, and he has just walked all over me for the past two years. Well let's face it, the last fifteen years at least.

After 20 minutes of fuming, I'm close to tears. I always cry when I'm angry, and it makes people think I'm the teary little woman. Over emotional. My phone rings and Ben's voice seems a bit more calm. "Emma, what's going on?"

"David didn't pick the boys up, so I rang him and he's cancelled," I blurt out.

"I could have had more notice! So he's just not going to bother then?"

"You had just as much notice as me. I can't exactly force him to come and get them. And what kind of message does that send to my kids? Neither of their parents want them." I let out a little whimper and the tears start to fall. I just can't stop them.

"I'm sorry, I don't mean to take my frustration out on you." He thinks for a minute. "Look the boys are old enough to be left in the house. I can still come and take you out for dinner, just an hour or so. Please Emma, I really need to see you and I don't want to leave you there upset."

"I'm not upset, I'm angry!" Okay honestly, I am upset too, I'm devastated.

"I don't want to leave you there angry then." He gives a little laugh, like he can't believe I can get angry.

I think for a bit, maybe he's right. Maybe I can leave them, they are old enough to be unsupervised. "Let me sort them out, can you give me an hour?" I finally say. He agrees and I hang up. I have a plan formulating. I can leave the boys for a few hours, get their food sorted first. It sounds obvious but although David cancelling is not new, having plans really is new to me.

I rush round, telling Josh and Noah about the change of plans. They don't seem to be bothered. I read them the riot act. No fighting, no messing about, call me if you need me, I'll not be long. I dish up their meal and run upstairs. I put my new dress on – a flowing flowery number, short sleeves and ruffled V neck. The dress skims my knees. It's a bit shorter than my usual. Okay, let's be honest, I don't have a usual. And my new shoes make my legs look longer and give me the extra height I need.

I see the headlights of Ben's car turn into the drive and immediately roll my eyes. It's not his Lamborghini, it's a bigger car, but it's still a Porsche. He doesn't get the chance to get out and knock because I rush outside and jump in as if it's a getaway car.

"Drive!" He laughs and reverses out of the drive.

We drive a few streets out of the neighbourhood and Ben signals and pulls in. He turns to face me.

"Hi," he says, staring at me.

"Hi yourself." I smile back at him and all the stress from the last few hours drains away.

"I've really missed you! And you look beautiful by the way." But he is the one who is beautiful. I can't believe this man is actually here and with me. His voice just makes me want to melt. "I've played it safe and have gone for Italian, it's not far from here." He looks at me again with lust in his eyes and he leans in and kisses me. I take a breath and he kisses me again.

"So you brought the none-flashy car then?" I roll my eyes.

"It's the least flashy car I have," he answers.

"We better get going or we'll miss our reservation," I say, when in all truth, I would be quite happy sitting here with him.

We get to a lovely restaurant and are seated in a small booth near the back. It's a romantic atmosphere, all dim lighting and candles. Ben makes a point of sitting beside me rather than opposite and I can feel the heat of his body through his clothes. His blue shirt has the first two buttons of the collar open with the rest of the buttons straining slightly with the hardness of his toned abs. I can just imagine kissing my way down his neck and opening every button. I shake my head trying to get my thoughts back to reality.

We have a lovely meal, but to be honest I barely notice it. We chat about work and life, and it all feels so natural that time just flies. We laugh about our friends and the daft things they get up to. We steer clear of the subject of me nearly cancelling the date. He can tell I don't want to talk about it and I think he is mindful to not let the circumstances ruin or cut short the evening.

Ben pays the bill and we head out to the car. He comes round to the passenger side and I think he's going to be a gentleman and open the door, but he changes his mind. He turns me and backs me up against the door. He leans in close and my breath hitches in anticipation. Cupping my jaw, his lips brush mine and the electricity I felt the first time he kissed me comes through loud and clear. He looks into my eyes for the green light to continue. How could I possibly want this to end? He kisses me again, teasing my lips open and rubbing his tongue with mine. It starts off slow, but the momentum grows with each motion. A kiss like this is a killer blow for someone who is wanting to keep a clear head. A kiss like this only leads to one thing and my spine tingles with desire. I'm wondering if he has noticed that my nipples have pebbled in my bra. I'm glad that he has his other hand around my waist because I think my knees may just give way. It seems like my body is starting to wake up and I feel so aroused.

I come to my senses and pull away. "We've got to get back," I say, knowing I'm just hurting myself, cutting things short.

"Okay." His expression is something between frustrated and understanding. He opens the door to let me inside and heads around the car to the driver's side. He pulls out of the car park and drives off. He rests his hand on my thigh, making circular motions with his thumb on my bare skin. Each stroke sends sparks through my body and I fizz with desire as we head back in silence. I bite my lip to stop any embarrassing sounds come out of my mouth.

As we get closer to my house he looks at me then back to the road. "I take it you don't want to say our goodbyes on your driveway!"

"That would be a bad idea." Could you imagine catching your mother making out with her boyfriend in the front seat of the car? It would definitely give the neighbours something to gossip about. "There is a country park not far from here. We could say goodbye there and then you can drop me at the end of my road."

"That sounds like a plan." He follows my directions and a few turns later we pull into a parking spot and he turns off the engine.

He waits for a moment then turns around in his chair and looks at me straight on. He smiles and says, "I am booked into my hotel until Sunday, so if you want to meet up, I'm here. If you can't, that's fine too. Whatever is easiest for you." He pauses to gauge my reaction. "But understand this," he says firmly, "I very much DO want to see you, more than anything." It's like he can read my overthinking mind.

I smile back at him. I'm not used to a man putting my needs first and the last statement put no doubt in my mind that he's here for me, and only me. "Okay, I would love to see you too. I'll just need to sort a few things."

There's a big smile on his face again, it lights up his eyes. "Great! Now can I get that goodbye?" He leans forward to kiss me, This time, though, it's not gentle, it's pure lust. His hand creeps up the inside of my thigh, his thumb stroking my skin. Oh god I can't remember ever being this turned on. The anticipation of his touch has got me at fever pitch and I break away from his kiss, panting.

His fingers move further up underneath my dress and skim the delicate lace fabric of my pants. "Okay?" he asks, but I can't get anything coherent out of my mouth, so I nod and bite my lip. He resumes the kiss and I give a little moan into his mouth. I don't know where it came from, my body just seems to be taking over. I can't even blame it on the drink, because I barely touched mine.

He pulls away again. "These need to come off!" He skims his fingers over the fabric of my knickers once more. At this point I would do anything he said, which feels dangerous but hot.

I stare at him for a minute, my brain trying to do a quick risk assessment. I push my hands up to my hips under my dress, hook the side of the pants and pull them down, lifting slightly to get them over my bum. I pull them over my knees and wriggle them to the floor and over my heels. I pick them up and he is waiting with his hand stretched out for them.

"I will need those for later." And puts them in his trouser pocket. It takes me a few seconds to realise what he means and when it dawns, the heat of arousal runs through me from my head, right to my feet.

He turns himself back to face me and starts the kiss again. His fingers have now reached the top of my legs and are rubbing me before pushing in between my delicate folds. He pulls away from the kiss and I gasp as his fingers stroke over me. I'm holding my breath, I'm so glad the girls forced me to get a bikini wax the other day.

His mouth is up to my ear. I can feel his warm breath.

"Oh Emma, you're so wet. Is that for me?" I still have no words and just nod. He gently kisses from my ear down to my collar bone. He pulls away and gently pulls my hips further forward towards the edge of the seat. He hooks my leg over towards the gear stick, opening me up. I let him. He is in full control.

This is a first for me and I have mixed emotions, a million things running through my head. I feel so turned on but also vulnerable at the same time. I feel like a naughty teenager in her boyfriend's car, wanting so much to have this experience, also apprehensive about being caught. Ben's gaze makes me feel safe and confident and he leans back in to kiss me again. Soft, gentle, individual kisses. He starts to rub again and moves his two fingers down until they reach my entrance. As he dips inside, I hear another moan and it seems to be coming from me. I'm panting while he continues and starts a trail of kissing and licking down my neck. His fingers slide all the way in and as he bends them my back arches. Each in and out motion has an effect on my body, like he's communicating directly with it. I have never felt anything like this before. It's so hot and I'm so turned on that I feel like my whole body is throbbing.

His hot breath is on my ear again. "You are so sexy Emma. I think you are amazing." With every word he says I can feel a pool of arousal getting bigger and bigger at the bottom of my stomach. "You feel so good, so tight and hot." A little whimper comes out and my body goes tense. I hold my breath again. "Don't hold back Emma, give it to me." It's more of a command than a request. "Let go Emma. I want to feel you come on my fingers." With that, I let out a loud moan and my body explodes. My mind goes completely blank, my body starts to shake and I only just remember to breathe. He pulls out of me, puts his finger in his mouth and sucks. "Good girl! You taste amazing!"

Before I even get my breath back, he's pulling me over to his seat to straddle him, my knees either side of his legs. As I lower myself I feel he is rock hard, straining the fabric of his trousers. He wriggles my hips so I'm in just the right position for me to rub against his erection. He tilts his head so our foreheads touch. "You good? You haven't said much." He pulls back to see my reaction. Both of his hands are on my ass, moving me gently backwards and forwards, carefully avoiding the steering wheel.

"I'm more than good!" I say as I remember how to speak. We smile, gazing at each other. With each movement I can feel him getting harder and the arousal building again. He pulls my chin down to make our mouths meet. My head feels fuzzy like I'm drunk, but I must be drunk on him.

The moment is lost by the sound of ringing. As I pull myself back to reality, I realise what I'm doing and where I am. I reach over and pull my phone out of my bag to see Noah's name flash up on the screen. Trying to steady my breathing and sound normal, I answer.

"What's up Noah?" I say trying to keep it together, as if he might be able to hear what we've been doing.

"Mum, when are you getting home? Josh made himself a pizza and forgot about it in the oven and now the kitchen is full of smoke." I manoeuvre myself back onto my seat and look at Ben with a pained expression. The moment is well and truly lost and I've gone from new, sexy Emma and back to mum in the blink of an eye.

"Have you turned the cooker off and opened a window?" I mouth *sorry* to Ben and he shrugs sympathetically. "I'm already on my way home, I'll only be a few minutes. Don't cook anything else!" I hang up and blow out the breath I've been holding in. We both put our seatbelts on in silence. Ben starts the engine and pulls out of the car park. Before I can comprehend what just happened, we are outside my house. I unhook the seatbelt, peck Ben on the cheek and get out of the car as if nothing has happened. I get to the front door and as I open it, I turn to see Ben speed off.

And here I am, back to reality.

Chapter Nine

Ben

I'm back in my hotel room, alone. It's not quite how I imagined this evening would end. I was furious when Emma's ex-husband dropped her in it with no notice. Seems like it's not the first time and won't be the last. He seems like a complete prick and he'll no doubt get worse when he finds out that Emma is seeing someone.

I don't know what it is about this woman. I've walked away from girls with less baggage because it was too much hard work. But with Emma, I can't stop thinking about her. I want to spend every minute in her company. She makes me want to please her in any way I can and that's totally not like me. I never do the chasing, but here I am waiting for her to message or call, or anything really, like a needy school boy.

I just loved the way we chatted tonight, when her smile lit up her face. Her little snort laugh that she tries to rein in. The fact that she is intelligent and sexy but doesn't even realise. In the back of my mind, I wondered whether Sean was right and she was just an itch I needed to scratch, but that's definitely not the case. I haven't even thought about my own needs. I just want to get her off so that I can see her face when she comes, and I'm desperate to be the only one that gives her pleasure.

I've been painfully hard all night, so I came in and went straight for a cold shower, thinking of Emma, and the way she came so hard for me had me jerking off to get some relief. Then when I got out and remembered I had her pants in my pocket, I had to do it again while they were in my hand. But she felt so good, I need another taste of her and I'm just desperate to get inside her. To see her face when I slide in, to hear her breath hitch and her skin pink up along her neck.

My phone buzzes with a message and I shoot up, eager to get it.

Emma: I'm really sorry about tonight!

I pick up the phone and dial her number without a second thought. There's no chance of playing it cool.

"Hi." She answers and her voice is all honey and velvet as I remember the way she moaned. What I wouldn't do to get her to moan my name.

"Why are you sorry? You have nothing to apologise for." I have a tone of annoyance, but only because she's always apologising for someone else's actions and it's not fair on her. I change my tone and start to tease her. "I'm not sorry for how quickly I made you come, or for how hard you make me." She giggles and I know that I have lightened the mood.

"Well, I am sorry that I had to leave you early. I am not sorry about the orgasm I had."

"Me either." I have playful Emma back. I like her. She's all giggly and fun. "I'm not sorry that I can still taste you."

"I'm not sorry that I may have left my mark on your flashy car's upholstery!" she laughs back.

"I'm not sorry that I have jerked off with your pants tonight."

"Please wash them before you give them back"

"Who says I'm giving them back?" There's the sound of shouting in the background and she mutters under her breath. I know we are on borrowed time and this phone call will be cut short, so I change the subject. "Have you thought about tomorrow? Because I need you in my bed at some point."

"I have thought but it doesn't mean I have the answers. Just leave it with me and I'll see what I can do."

"Don't let him take the piss out of you" I say sternly. I think I've overstepped a bit and it could go either way. I wait for her reaction.

She huffs. "He'll take the piss no matter what happens, it's in his nature. I just need to... I don't know, react differently I guess." There's more background noise. "For fuck's sake, I'm gonna have to go. I'll speak to you tomorrow. Sweet dreams," she says with a giggle.

"Oh I will, because I'll be dreaming of you." She groans at the cheesiness. "Too much?" I ask.

"A bit! Bye!"

And with that I feel totally elated and can't stop the grin I have plastered on my face. I need to distract myself or I'll spend the night jerking off looking at her photo. I get up and root through my bag for my gym gear. I need to get rid of this energy somehow.

Chapter Ten

Emma

I'm undecided whether to message David to ascertain his plans for tomorrow, or just bypass him altogether. Either way could cause problems. So I message Lizzie to see if the boys can have a sleep over at hers. We used to do it a lot when they were younger but I'm not sure how that will work with Joshua and Sienna being 15 and now incapable of talking to the opposite sex. I'll have to remind them that between the ages of two and seven neither of them would contemplate going to the toilet without the other.

I also can't leave Josh alone in the house after last night. My nerves just can't take it. Maybe I should have started giving them more independence earlier on. But I'm desperate to see Ben. To see where, if we had not been interrupted, things would have gone next. I'm also not sure if he'd want to make the effort again if I don't manage to spend time with him. I think he's a good guy but I'm so out of the game I can't trust my own judgement.

The boys are sorted and dropped off with Lizzie. She has told me I must turn my phone off and she'll deal with anything that comes up. I love that woman. She's one of the handful of people I trust with my kids, no questions asked.

Ben has messaged me the address of his hotel, some fancy country house hotel a few miles away. He wanted to come and pick me up, but I just know that something will happen to ruin our plans. I've packed an overnight bag and I've left the one thing I wanted to avoid until last, to ring David. What do I tell him? Should I ask him when he's getting the kids or just tell him straight off Lizzie has them. I'm going to have to gauge what kind of mood he's in first, I suppose.

I always feel like I'm on the back foot with him and it raises my anxiety levels. I take two deep breathes and press the call button and wait. But it goes straight to answer machine. I panic, that wasn't the scenario I had running through my mind. When the beep comes I just blurt out where the kids are staying, hang up and turn off my phone. I feel like a naughty kid.

I put my bag in the boot and get in the driver's seat, turn the engine on and type in the postcode of the hotel. It's only five miles from mine, but it might as well be a different country. I pull out of the drive and follow the route the car gives me. I won't relax until I get there. I always feel like my plans are going to be disrupted at the last minute. It's generally why I make very few plans.

I eventually turn left, through the big gates and up the long driveway adorned with thick oak trees. Pulling into the car park, you can tell by the cars that this place is nice. The kind of place I haven't been to in a long time. It's the kind of place Sammy would treat us all to for a spa day. Even BC, which stands for Before Children, we'd not have been able to afford something this opulent for a night away.

I get out of the car, my stomach full of butterflies. I decide to leave my bag behind for now and make my way up the stone steps to the big front door. Through the door you can immediately see the expense of the place. The lobby is all high ceilings, chandeliers and huge paintings. I'm glad I dressed up a bit for this with my sleeveless floaty dress, buttoned around the back of my neck, matched with a blazer and Ben's favourite heels. Jeans would not cut it for this place.

I make my way to the oversized oak reception desk. Ben told me to ask for him, making it feel more like a business meeting. I get the receptionist's attention.

"Hi, I'm here to see Ben Ambrose." She smiles politely and I'm wondering whether she's judging me already.

"Can I take your name please."

"Yes, it's Emma Lowther." And now I'm fidgeting, thinking she might tell me to get out because I don't belong here.

She gives me a grin as if she knows something I don't. "Ah Ms Lowther, Mr Ambrose has asked that you meet him in the drawing room for afternoon tea."

"Okay then," I say looking round.

"I'll take you through." She comes round to my side of the desk. She's very smart, well dressed and professional looking, with her hair in a tight bun.

I follow her through the lobby, looking up the sweeping stairs that connect with a balcony, where you can look down onto the seating area. We walk through a door and my attention is immediately drawn to the light. There are huge windows all around the room, looking out onto lawns and gardens that seem never ending. But my attention is drawn to the man sitting at a table in the corner. He looks relaxed, sitting with his head down looking at his phone. As if he senses me there, he lifts his head and smiles, putting his phone in his pocket. We walk over to his table and he doesn't break my eye contact.

"Ms Lowther!" he says with a grin.

"Mr Ambrose!" I say, looking amused. It's all very Pride and Prejudice. The receptionist looks between both of us and Ben speaks to her without taking his eyes off me.

"Thank you, Kirsty!" I don't hear if she replies, but I notice she's left and I'm still just standing there looking at Ben. "Would you like to sit down?" I have to shake myself out of it, but he's all consuming. I sit down opposite him.

"Afternoon Tea? I thought you would have met me in your room."

"I thought it better we had something to eat first. Once I get you upstairs, I'll just want you naked." I blush, I did wonder if we'd just rip each other's clothes off.

I take my seat and look back over to where the receptionist disappeared. "You charmed another young lady I see!" I laugh

"Is anyone immune to you?" His smile drops and he sits up straight.

"There's only one lady I want to charm!" A waiter comes over and places a cake stand down, tiered with sandwiches and cakes. "I didn't know what you wanted to drink," he says, changing his focus. "Tea, coffee or Prosecco?"

"I think I better stick with tea." The waiter nods and goes back into the kitchen.

"So I know I probably already asked this when we first met, but humour me! What do you do to earn enough to have those flashy cars?"

He gives a little laugh, he's probably told me, but I was too drunk to remember. "Well I have a property development company, I make money buying properties and renovating them, then selling them on."

"Ok so it's your company? You don't work for anyone else?"

"That's right, Ambrose Holdings."

"Ah okay! Rewind that and start at the beginning. Tell me how it started, because you are still so young."

"This feel a bit like an interview." He fidgets in his chair but I just shrug it off. "Okay, so I was at university and it was the spring at the end of my second year. My Nan died and left me some money." A sadness pulls over his face for a moment. "I was close to my Nan and I wanted to use it to do something substantial. I bought a property. It was really run down and I did it up, mainly myself and a few friends. Then I sold it for a profit, which I used to buy the next one. And so it began."

"Nice! A bit of hard labour never did anyone any harm," I say.

"I decided that I was better off dropping out of university and focusing on the business."

"Risky move! Did you think about finishing university first and that way you'd have something to fall back on? What did your parents say?" I'm aware that it was a very *mum* thing to say.

"My parents weren't really in the picture and I was in my early twenties and knew better. But I'm not daft, I knew my Nan would have expected me to finish my degree, so once the business was established, I finished the course."

"Wow!" He really is smart. "So how much is the business worth now?" I realise that was a rude question to ask. "Sorry, you don't need to answer that!"

"I'm not sure the figure would impress you, you don't seem that bothered by money."

"I'm not. There's more to life than money." Says someone who isn't a multimillionaire.

But it's true, it really doesn't impress me at all. I've known beautiful souls who haven't had a penny to their name, but I have also known those from money who are complete dicks!

"There is indeed. But the main thing is that I love what I do, I work with my friends and I can buy a new flashy car when I want to." He sniggers.

"So tell me about your friends? The ones from the bar!"

"Yes, the ones you met, they are some of my closest. Sean is my managing director, he's been with me from the start. We went to university together and did stupid shit. Joel, the geeky shy one, he's my accountant. He is very smart but socially awkward. And Piers, well I don't work with him anymore, but he worked for the bank that I got my first business loan from and we've been friends ever since." We take a pause from the interrogation and he selects something else to eat. "What about you?" he asks eventually. "You told me you and Sammy are friends from university and I obviously know where you work."

"Yes, how exactly did you know where to send those flowers?" I say narrowing my eyes at him. He laughs it off.

"Oh I'm first level stalker, I'll have you know."

I laugh out loud at his confession. "Thought as much!" I continue. "Well I went to university, with Sammy of course, got a Marketing degree. Sammy went off to a swanky job with some law firm in Edinburgh, hence why we were there. My other friends, Beth and Megan, I work with, and Lizzie is a mummy friend." I explain.

"So go back to the university and job part. Tell me about that. Are you doing marketing for the haulage firm?"

"Well no, not really. The company I work for are so pre-historic they don't think they need a marketing strategy, so I basically do admin."

"How come? If you have a marketing degree, was that what you wanted to do when you left Uni?"

"Well yes but I met David, my ex, in my final year and I honestly don't know what happened from then. I think looking back I took a job on the first rung of the ladder. I was wanting to work my way up, but I think David's career was put above my own." I shrug. It's the first time I've really revisited the direction my life has taken. "We decided to get married and then we had the boys. I had to work part-time because of child care. And just stayed at my current job." It makes me feel quite sad looking back.

I blow out a breath, I realise I put my own life on the back burner for everyone else, but I didn't realise just how much I had sacrificed. "And now here I am, hurtling towards forty, divorced, trying to manage teenage boys, which I can tell you, is harder than having toddlers. I'm constantly managing everyone else, still!" We don't talk for a few minutes. I may have just scared him off, but it's the truth.

"So! If you could do anything, or be anywhere, where would it be?" he asks.

"Honestly? I have absolutely no idea." I let out another sigh. "I think this conversation has got a little too heavy. Can we change the subject?" My insecurities have surfaced again. I think a little part of me should have been more forceful in what I wanted, in the beginning of my marriage, and not be so scared to stretch my legs.

"Okay." He thinks for a bit. "Do you sleep naked or do you wear pyjamas?"

I nearly choke on the tea I'm trying to sip! This man is a funny mix. He's so easy to talk to, I feel so comfortable chatting, but then the next minute, when he gazes at me with that glint in his eye, he makes me feel like a teenager again, all shy and stuttery.

"Definitely pyjamas," I say, eyes raised.

We finish eating and continue talking, but now I am three pots of tea in and need the toilet. I excuse myself and head to the restrooms. When I come back out and find my bearings, I look towards the reception desk and see a familiar figure – David.

He's standing at the desk, looking smart but casual and he's with some skinny, blonde woman, who has to be almost twenty years his junior. He's a walking cliché, his arm around her waist. I rush back into the drawing room and over to our table.

"We've got to make a move!" I say in a panicky voice.

"Is everything okay?"

"No I've just seen David at the front desk."

"Has he found out where you are?"

"No, and I'm pretty sure he won't want me knowing he's here either." I look back to the doorway I came through as they are being led in. Ben stands and grabs my hand to angle himself behind, shielding me from their view as he manoeuvres us to the exit, out into the courtyard and round to the next door leading back in.

My mind flips between not wanting to be seen, to being furious that David is here, and back again.

"And here's me worried he would be upset about not being with the boys!"

"Let's just get upstairs and out of the way. Then you can have your meltdown in private." His words are harsh, but absolutely fair.

Ben is clearly pissed off with the situation, but I can't work out if he's upset for me or with me. We rush up the stairs and I glance over the balcony but they're out of sight. We reach a door and Ben opens it and moves aside, gesturing for me to enter. I storm through the door and throw my handbag on the chair and the ranting starts.

"How could he?" I start. "The absolute piece of shit, selfish bastard. He'd rather be out with some bimbo than spend some time with his children."

"Emma!" Ben puts his hands on my shoulders as if he is going to shake me out of my anger. "I don't want to talk about him!" He looks down at me but the anger that I caught before has gone as he takes in my conflicted expression. "But if you need to get this out and have a rant... well just go for it!" Just looking at him, all the anger washes away. I must have looked like a psycho. He didn't sign up for all this baggage, but yet, he's here for me. I let out a little laugh and his face turns to puzzled amusement. "So it's funny now? I thought you were going to start throwing things!"

"So did I." I break away from him and realise where I am. "Wow! This place is amazing" I look round the room. It's huge with ceiling to floor windows on two walls, covered with heavy plush drapes. The room is divided up into lounge areas, dining, work and bedroom. It has the most beautiful sleigh bed on the other side of the room, with a long velvet throw at the bottom and a multitude of pillows of all shapes and sizes.

The furniture is antique and in keeping with the building. I walk over to the en-suite, which is classic but modern, with granite surfaces, double sink and double shower. The best bit is the huge standalone bath. The bathroom is probably the same size as my living room.

I head back into the living area where Ben has taken a bottle of fizz out of an ice bucket, ready to pop. I walk over and pick up the two champagne flutes. "What are we toasting to?" I ask as the cork pops and Ben fills up the glasses.

Ben shrugs, "I don't know? Maybe a toast to not being inter-rupted?"

"Yeah! Cheers to that." I hand him a glass and clink mine on his. I take a sip then let out a breath.

The realisation that I'm in a hotel room, with a very gorgeous younger man suddenly dawns and I'm nervous again. He takes my drink from me, puts both glasses on the table and comes back towards me. He slips my blazer over my shoulders until it falls away from me. He leans in, wrapping his hand around the back on my neck and kisses me slowly.

"Okay wait." I say, pulling away. "I'm not sure I can have sex in the middle of the day."

"What do you mean?" He looks perplexed.

"Well it's too light. You'll see all my flaws and squishy bits." I feel so vulnerable in this room with him and fold my arms around my middle. I really fancy him, he makes my body heat up. I can't think straight when he is near, but also what if he thinks I'm some flabby, boring, old mummy? I haven't had sex in such a long time, and I really don't remember anything other than boring, wait-until-the-kids-are-asleep, sex.

"What you think are flaws, I think are…"

I interrupt before he can placate me. "I'm not as experi-enced as you. I'm not used to having hot, steamy in-the-mid-dle-of-the-day sex. In fact, I can't remember the last time I had sex at all."

"Princess, you are overthinking this! If you don't want to do this now, that's fine."

"I didn't say that!"

"What will make you more comfortable? A blindfold?"

"If the blindfold is on you, then yes, maybe."

He laughs out loud. "That is not going to happen! I want to see every last bit of you. I want to kiss every inch, I want to touch you, so I know what every bit of you feels like. That includes every line, every wobbly bit, every perfect imperfection."

"Every stretch mark?"

"Yes, every stretch mark!" he says. "You are focusing on your body, and I get that you feel a little insecure about it. So why don't you focus on mine instead."

"Okay!" I draw out and look at him quizzically.

"Well then, keep your clothes on until YOU want to take them off. You are in control, you touch me, you undress me, and I'll keep my hands to myself. When you want me to touch you, you'll have to direct me. You're in charge."

I take in a big deep breath. "Okay!" I take a step closer to him and open up his jacket. I run my two hands up his torso and over his pecs. He is so sculpted, like marble but with a warmth. I push up over his shoulders to push the jacket off him and down his arms until it falls to the floor. I start to unfasten the buttons on his shirt one by one, from the top down, revealing his neck. He smells unbelievable. His cologne is warm and spicy. Unbuttoning more unveils his six pack and as I open his shirt up my thumbs run across his skin. His chest has a dusting of dark hair with a trail that disappears into the top of his trousers.

All this time he has never taken his eyes off me. I move around him, trailing my hands on his skin to take the shirt from his back. He is just as magnificent from the rear. He has muscles where I never knew you could. He's muscly but not pumped. He looks like he takes care of himself but isn't a body builder. I run both hands down his back in appreciation and when I move forward and brush my lips along the back of his shoulder. I hear him take in a sharp breath. It's good to know my touch affects him, as much as his affects me.

He still hasn't reached out to touch me, so I know he is keeping his word, but I'm not sure how long I can keep up initiating touch as it's so unfamiliar. I step back around in front of him and start to undo the buttons at the back of my neck, unfastening my dress, and reach down to pull it over my head. He takes me in for a minute. I think he appreciates that matching black lace balcony bra and lace pants.

I step closer to him and reach for his hands that are itching to touch and pull them around me. He steps even closer and spreads his hands out to get as much skin contact as possible. I pull my arms round his neck, looking up into his eyes. Even in heels there is a height difference between us and I push myself up so my lips reach his. The desire in his eyes is on another level. He slightly pulls back from me and angles his head to get better access. But the spell is broken by a loud noise. It takes a few seconds to register that it's the phone in the corner of the room.

He pulls back from me and looks to the ceiling. "You have got to be fucking kidding me." I let out a little laugh, disappointed at the break from him, but relieved that this time it wasn't me.

He stalks over to the phone muttering as he goes and answers with a curt "YES!". There's a pause while someone on the other end speaks. "Is it urgent? ... Right! I'm on my way." He looks up at me, clearly annoyed by what he has been told. "Something has happened to my car, they won't say exactly what, but I need to go and check it out." He picks his shirt up and pulls it on, buttoning it up I can see the frustration in his face. He looks up at me, "I'm sorry!" The anger has gone.

"It's fine." I say with a little smile, it's really nice being the one on the receiving end of the apologies for once. "While you're there can you get my bag from my boot?"

"Of course."

"It's the grey..."

He cuts me off.

"I know which car is yours!"

"Of course you do... stalker!" He gives a little chuckle as I hand him the keys, then pulling them back before he grabs them, I say, "or do you already have your own set?"

"Okay, I'm not that bad"

"Yet!" He gives me a quick kiss on the lips and heads out of the door.

"I won't be long!" The door closes behind him. I take a moment to look around the room, wondering what to do, feeling a bit vulnerable in just my underwear. I contemplate finding my phone and switching it on, but that could open up a whole other can of worms.

The room phone rings again and I go over to answer it. Ben's voice comes through, sounding agitated. "Em? It's gonna take longer than I expected. Someone has broken into my car, but I'll be as quick as I can."

"Oh no!" I answer. "Just get it sorted out. Don't worry about me, I might have a bath while I'm waiting."

I don't know how long it takes before Ben comes back into the room. I'm laying with my head over the end of the bath tub, the room full of steam. It's been really nice having a bath in such a lovely, deep, bubbly water, without the interruption of my phone, doorbell, or the boys asking me random questions through the door. There's a faint knock.

"Can I come in?" He's back.

"Yes sure." I answer and he opens the door and steps into the bathroom.

"Well, you look all relaxed." He smiles down at me.

"You don't. what's happened?"

He rubs his hand over his face. "I'm not quite sure. The back windscreen has been smashed and it looks like someone has bumped the rear passenger side because the lights are smashed. The passenger door was opened, and everything from the glove compartment has been pulled out, but nothing was taken." His face portrays his annoyance.

"Sounds a bit odd. Have the police been?"

"No. The reception staff said they would deal with the police for me because they won't be out for hours, if at all. They're pulling up any CCTV they have of the carpark too. They said it's rare for them to have any break ins to cars, and if there are, there's usually no damage, just things taken."

"Oh God, you don't think this has anything to do with seeing David, do you?" The thought makes me shudder. Would David go out of his way to damage Ben's car? Did he even see me here?

"Well I did wonder, but I don't think he saw you, plus he doesn't know me or the car I drive, so I can't see how it could be." His brows crease. "And if he had seen your car, I would have thought he would have targeted that, but I checked it over when I got your bag." He pulls a face as if he's trying to think things through but can't get an answer. Then he looks at me and smiles, realising where we both are again. "Can I join you?"

"That'd be nice." I reply, and he ducks back into the bedroom to retrieve our glasses of fizz. He places them beside the free-standing bath and starts to undress. I move forward as he steps in behind me and as he sits down, the water spills over the side.

"Jeez, this bath is as hot as the sun!" He settles down and I lean back to rest my head on his torso.

"I like it hot!" I say, laughing as I realise what I have said.

"Good to know!" He chuckles as he kisses my ear. I feel his body start to relax and he picks up the glasses and passes me mine. I can't comprehend how nice this is feels. I'm so relaxed. I don't know whether it's the heat and steam of the essential oils from the bath, or that this man makes me feel something I haven't felt in a long time.

For someone that I have known only a short amount of time he makes me feel safe, relaxed and sure of myself. I'm used to feeling on edge around the men in my life.

He gently strokes his hand up and down my side. It's nice but with every touch I can feel a tingle reach up my legs and pool at the bottom of my spine. He's not completely unaffected either, I can tell. His erection gets harder on my back the longer we lie there. He breaks the silence first.

"Although I'm loving this right now, I think we need to get out before it gets too cold for you, and probably the right temperature for me!" He's right. I'm turning into a prune as we speak.

I lean forward, and he steps out first, grabs a white fluffy towel with one hand and he offers me the other hand as help to get out of the bath. Once I'm out he wraps me up in a bundle, so I can't escape the kiss he presses on my lips. Teasing my mouth open he deepens the kiss, rubbing his tongue over mine.

He walks me backwards into the main room, not breaking the kiss until the back of my legs hit the arm chair next to the bed. "This time, Ms Lowther, I want to taste you for longer," he says, his tone dropped, sounding more seductive than ever. He unwraps me from the towel and pushes me down onto the chair. It's then I get a full-frontal sight of him, and wow, he looks impressive. But I have a slight panic, wondering how I'm going to take something of that size.

I want to feel him in my hands, but before I can touch him he leans towards me and trails kisses down my body as he goes to kneel. As he reaches my breasts, he kisses around, and then takes my now hard nipple into his mouth and gives it suck, his tongue swirling around the peak. With that one action a shot of electricity shoots to my core. I let out a gasp and I can feel his mouth turn into a smile on my skin. He moves to the other nipple and has the same effect, my back arching away from the chair.

He continues his trail of kisses down my body until he gets to my navel. Putting his hands on my hips he pulls me to the edge of the chair so I'm in more of a half-laying position. My body has totally taken over. I'm panting, and I can't stop myself. He sits back on his heels and starts the journey in the opposite direction, kissing the bottom of my foot, then my ankle and all up the inside of one leg, using his hands on my knees to open up my legs. He stops short of the place I need him and starts on the other leg. When he finally gets to the top, he looks up at me.

"Open up for me Emma!" It's an order and I look down at him, unsure of myself all of a sudden. "Be a good girl!" I don't answer, I just let my legs go loose and he pushes them apart.

I can't form any words just now, my head is spinning.

"You are so perfect." He directs his comment directly to my throbbing centre. With one sweeping motion he leans in and licks me from the bottom to the top, over my clit, and I nearly jump out of the chair, a burst of wetness escaping me. He holds my legs in place so I can't move, and he does it again. I let out a moaning sound that I never even knew I had inside of me. "You taste amazing!" The mixture of his touch and his words have my back arching away from the chair again. I'm panting as he licks again, smaller licks concentrating on the big bundle of nerves ready to have a fit. My mind is completely blank. My body knows how this works with moans and gasps escaping from me. I flex my hips to get his mouth closer each time.

I feel on the edge, as he puts one finger, then two, inside me, crooking them forward to hit a spot that I never realised I had, and starts to move in and out. I hold my breath as the heat pools at my spine, wetness runs down the inside of my thighs. With another lick I go off like a firework. I've never moaned so loud.

"Oh my god!" I shout as my body convulses. My vagina pulses around his fingers and as I start to draw breath again, he pulls his fingers out slowly.

"Oh my god, you felt amazing coming on my fingers." He stands and pulls me to my feet. I hope he doesn't want me to walk anywhere because I feel like jelly. He turns us both round and sits on the chair, placing me on his lap, my legs straddled at either side of him. We are back to where we got interrupted yesterday.

We are face to face and I move closer to kiss him. I can taste myself on his lips. I break the kiss, still trying to catch my breath and I feel like I'm having some kind of out of body experience. I can honestly say I have never had an orgasm like that before.

I look down at him and he is rock hard, the tip glistening and pressed up to his stomach. I'm aching to feel him inside me.

"Are you ready for me?" he asks, and I really don't know whether my body can take him. But I know I am so desperate for it. I nod and he leans over to the table next to us and picks up a condom I never noticed before. He rips the packet open with is teeth and places it on his tip, his eyes roll back in his head as he pulls it down. "Okay?" he asks again looking back to me. I nod again. "I need to hear you say it!" he says through gritted teeth as he strokes his cock.

"Yes, I'm good," is all I can manage. And with that green light he kisses me deeply, stoking his tongue through my mouth, my lust reaching fever pitch. He indicates for me to lift up as he holds himself at the base to angle himself towards my entrance. As he's lined up, he pushes me down onto him for the first few inches. I moan and we both still to give me some time to become accustomed to his size.

"Fucking hell, you feel amazing." He sounds breathless, my head rolls back as a flush runs from my toes all the way up to the top of my head. "So tight! But you need to relax, let me in a bit more." He moves his mouth to my nipples again and gives one a suck. I feel another rush of moisture covering him, making it easier for him to move further inside me.

I feel myself stretch to accommodate him and I wince a little. He stops himself, looks deep into my eyes and without needing to ask the question I nod my answer. He puts his hands on my hips, gently moving me back and forward. It means he's brushing over my clit each time. I moan needing more and as if we are communicating through grunts, he gives me more. Every time he hits that spot inside me, I let out a noise. The pleasure is building and I can barely keep myself together.

"If you keep making those little noises this will be over very quickly."

But I can't help the sounds coming out of me, they are pure pleasure. I have never had an orgasm through penetration alone so it comes as more of shock to me, than him, when I still and let out an "Oh Fuck!" as I explode around him.

"I need to move," he says as he stands, lifting me with him. He wraps my legs around him, still connected, and takes a few steps towards the bed. He drops us both down, my back hitting the mattress with a slight bounce. "I need to be deeper." I didn't think he could get any further in, but he manages it and starts to move with quick thrusts, I'm still pulsing around him.

I'm watching him as his mouth falls open. I can see in his facial expressions that he's on the edge. His thrusts speed up and with a grunt he explodes.

"Fuck! Fuck! fuck!" His eyes bore into mine. He slows to a stop and leans closer to give me a slow, sultry kiss on my lips. He slowly pulls out of me and discards the condom before collapsing down beside me. I lift up my head as he puts his arm around my neck.

"Well Ms Lowther, who knew you would be a multiple orgasm woman." We are both still trying to get our breath, flushed and sticky from sweat.

I chuckle. "Not me for sure, I'm as surprised as you. I don't usually get one."

"What?" He's lifted up to look at me in shock. "You know that means I'm trying for more next time?"

"Next time, eh?"

"Yes, give me ten minutes and I'll be ready."

"I won't! I can't feel my toes," I say laughing.

"We'll just have a little rest first." He kisses my cheek and I feel him relax.

I must have fallen asleep. As I blink myself awake, Ben is looking at me. "Hello there, sleepy head!"

"How long was I asleep?"

"About twenty minutes."

"And you've just laid there staring at me?"

"Yes!"

"Weird!"

"You were very cute."

"I doubt that!"

"Especially when you were snoring."

"I don't snore!" I look at him, affronted by the suggestion.

"Ok then... You just mew like a little kitten."

"Right! I can't stay here tonight if I snore." I go to get up and he makes a grab for me, slightly panicked.

"No, don't you dare... Okay you don't snore, and you do have to stay here with me."

I give off a little laugh. I think he thought I might be serious. "Well if I stay, what do you want to do tonight?"

"Isn't that obvious?" He raises his eyebrows and looks at me suggestively.

"NO!"

"But you're already naked, so that takes away one thing I want to do. I think, firstly, I'll lick you all over until you do that thing..." I cut him off.

"That's not what I meant. I was talking about dinner, going out, that kind of thing."

"Why? Are you hungry?"

"Not just yet, but I will be." I continue with my explanation. "I like to know what I'm doing or I get a bit anxious."

"Okay, I see, you're a planner then!" He's trying to work me out. "Let's look at some options. We could go out to a restaurant for dinner, or we could go to the restaurant downstairs or maybe we could stay naked and order room service."

I weigh up the options. I like that he's not dictating our every move. "Is it bad that I don't want to make the effort to get dressed and go out?"

"No, not at all!"

"Would you think I was needy if I said I wanted it to be just the two of us? I don't really want to share you." I grin.

"No that's perfect because I don't really like to share you either." He grins back at me.

"Room service it is then." He gets up and goes over to the desk to find the room service menu, giving me a full and uncensored view of his ass. I'm sure when I was a young, impressionable girl, I had a poster on my bedroom wall with this exact image.

He comes back over with the menu. "Then we can go back to my original plan and we'll still be naked."

"Very funny!" I say, smacking him with the menu as he gets back into bed. His phone lights up, but he doesn't make a move to answer it.

"Oh, I'm deadly serious!" He lunges over and grabs me, planting kisses all over while I try to fight him off.

Once he has given up and I've stopped laughing, I remind him of the incidents of the past few hours.

"Do you think you should check up on your car?" He looks at me like he's completely forgotten that his car was broken into. "Knowing our luck they'll ring when we're in a compromising position."

"True, I'll give reception a ring now." He rolls onto his side and picks up the phone next to the bed. He speaks to them briefly while I look at the menu. His phone lights up again and I glance over to where it lies on the bedside table. The name Ami is displayed. I frown but avert my eyes, I have no right to ask who he is getting calls from.

"What do you fancy?" I say, as he puts the phone down.

"You!" I pull the *not funny* face. "There's no news," he says, pointing to the phone. "I've asked them to deal with it and not to disturb us." He takes the menu off me. "I'm not bothered really. We could get a selection of things and share."

"I thought you said you didn't like to share?"

"I don't like to share YOU!"

"Then yes we could get a few different bits and have a bedroom picnic."

"Is that a thing?"

"Did you never do anything like that as a kid?"

"Not that I remember."

"We used to do a living room picnic when the boys were little, usually when they were being fussy with food or we couldn't be bothered to cook." I think for a minute. "I say we, I actually mean I!" I roll my eyes.

"Tell me a bit about your kids."

"Really? I'm sure you're not interested in my family."

"I'm interested in you, and they are your life. So yes, I am interested in them."

"I know but I bet you don't talk to your other dates about their kids." The insecurities start to kick in, talking about kids really is a mood killer.

"I don't think I have been on a date with anyone who has kids." He ponders.

"Well, that makes me feel really old. How old even are you?"

"I'm thirty, but I do usually hook up with women a bit younger."

"Less complicated I suppose!" I wonder again why he is hooking up with me. "And that makes me feel even older."

"How old are you then? You don't look a day older than 25."

"Thirty nine."

"Well you know what they say, you're only as old as the man you feel!"

"If that was the case, I would have been pregnant in high school." I roll my eyes again.

"So go on, tell me about them."

I take a deep breath. He'll find out about them eventually, so I may as well. "My eldest is Joshua and he's fifteen."

"Wow, so he'll be in the masturbating and porn stage then!"

"Oh my god, STOP! Why did you have to say that? These are my babies!" I put my head in my hands. This is not what a mother wants to hear.

"Sorry, I couldn't resist. But to be fair, I've been a teenage boy myself and I know what goes on behind closed doors."

"I said stop!" He puts his hands up as a surrender.

"Okay sorry! But you realise that makes you a MILF."

"Have you actually got out of the teenage boy phase yet?"

"Probably not! You were saying..." He encourages me to go on.

"So Josh is complicated. Doesn't go out much, plays on his computer, but also doesn't handle school well. I'm always getting called out of work because he's ill. He just can't cope with that kind of environment."

"That must be tough on you, juggling it all?"

"Yes it is. Thanks for acknowledging that, nobody usually does." I stroke his face and continue on. "And then there's Noah, he's thirteen and an absolute delight. But he's now retreated to his bedroom. DON'T SAY IT!" I hold up my finger, to silence him and it's not mentioned again. "Loves school, he's clever and likes to stick to the rules, does his homework on time, that kind of kid. But he doesn't do well with social situations with his peers. Ask him to go and do a job for a teacher and he's there. But ask him to make conversation with a group his own age and he just can't."

"But isn't that pretty normal for some kids at that age?"

"Who knows? I suppose in some ways. Maybe talking to girls, but he doesn't really have any friends as such."

"The split with their dad must have been difficult for them?"

"I thought we weren't allowed to talk about him?"

"We're not, we are talking about them."

"Okay, well I don't really know. We did the whole *Mummy and Daddy still love you very much, they just don't love each other* spiel. But looking back I don't think there was much change for the worse. *He who shall not be named* was very much an absent parent when we were together. You know the kind, working late at the office, nights out with the lads and so on.

"Do you know he even went on a lads' holiday when Noah was tiny and left me to it!" I sigh. "And when he was there, he was always picking faults with them and with me. So not much has changed there then."

"But at least you got out of that toxic relationship."

"Ironically, it was him who pulled the plug. And when you have children together you are never really out of a relationship in one form or another. Even if he is a complete prick!"

Ben laughs, but then gets all serious. "You realise that you are worth more than that, right?"

I shrug, "I'm beginning to, but you don't really notice what's happening until you decide not to put up with it anymore. I was choosing the quiet life with everything really. I just went with things to not cause any arguments or cause anymore anxiety. But I think I'm up for an argument now!"

"Not with me I hope!"

"No, I quite like you!"

"Oh do you now? At least you'll admit it now."

"Admit it? I never denied liking you."

"But it took some persuading for you to see me again."

"Like I said, *quiet life*!"

"I'm not trying to cause you any grief."

"I know, but what are you trying to do? Why did you want to persuade me?" I gesture between us. I need to know what his motives are.

"Are you kidding? Do you want me to write a list of the reasons I wanted to see you again? Because I will if it makes you realise how amazing you are?"

"I'm not asking you to boost my ego. I am genuinely curious. What is it about me that would make you drive hundreds of miles to be with me, without even a guarantee you will? I'm sure there are lots of beautiful, uncomplicated women in Edinburgh who would suit you better."

He thinks for a moment before answering. "There may well be, but none of them are you. I honestly can't explain it. I'm just drawn to you. As soon as you walked into that bar, I couldn't take my eyes off you. I watched you with your friends and you just look out for everyone else. You have a kind soul and it just radiates from you."

I'm absolutely gobsmacked. "And you got all that from me walking into a bar?"

"Well, no. We spent most of that night together. Although I know you don't remember much, which also doesn't do much for MY ego, that you can't remember how charming and witty I was."

"You must have been to get my number. I never give it out!"

"It must have been my amazing kissing as well, which you also don't remember, so I think I better remind you." He leans towards me and settles in for another long, electric kiss.

Chapter Eleven

Ben

The sound of my alarm brings me round and I quickly turn it off. I reach over for Emma but of course she isn't there, because I'm in my own bed and it's the Monday after the best weekend. I remember Sunday morning was a very different affair. I opened my eyes to see her laying there. She looked amazing, her eyes lids fluttering as is if she was in a dream, her hair splayed over the pillow. She looked so relaxed. I doubt she would be if she knew that the bedsheets were only covering her bottom half, but she looked like a goddess.

The weekend was way more than I had expected in many ways. It felt like she totally came out of herself and left all her baggage at the door. Although I have a sneaking suspicion her baggage is following us round. It's got to be some kind of coincidence that we saw her ex and my car also got broken into.

I can't see how it could have been him, but it all doesn't sit well with me.

We had the most amazing connection and being with her just felt so right. She's different from the girls I usually date and I'm different with her. I know some of it is because I haven't given myself to anyone else fully for a very long time.

We ordered room service on Saturday night, neither of us wanting to venture out or to share each other with anyone else. We sat on the bed in our hotel robes, eating a picnic of food, chatting laughing and messing about. We watched something on the TV, but I can't remember what it was. She is so easy to be with and she has no expectations of me. Not the money, not the status, not catching feelings or getting the best Instagram-able photo. She just wants us to spend time together. And I'm totally here for that. She is also, by far, the sexiest woman on the planet and I can't get enough of her.

We had fucked so many times I lost count. It was hard and fast, then it was slow and sweaty. We fucked in the shower and then a quick one when we woke up. Just thinking about how she looked when she was turned on has given me flash backs. She looks so amazing that I made her keep eye contact and it was in all honesty the best sex I can remember. I think I may be addicted to her. This obsession I have with her is unhealthy.

We went our separate ways on Sunday morning. She had to get back and her guilt had started to settle in. On the drive home she was all I could think about and that's not like me. I started imagining our life together. What if we could wake up together every morning?

But today I start the day without her, not knowing when the next time we'll get chance to meet up will be, or if we'll ever be able to do that again. I just don't know where her head is at. She is always doing for everyone else, so making plans is really hard. If this is going to become a thing, then I'll need to get used to it.

I pull myself out of bed and head to the shower. I turn on the shower but hear my phone ringing in the bedroom and head back to answer, willing it to be her.

"Morning lover boy!"

"Fuck off Sean, I'm getting in the shower." I hang up and continue to get ready, I have a feeling this is going to be a very long week.

Chapter Twelve

I'm sitting in our usual restaurant, waiting for Ami to show up, and as ever she is fashionably late. I'll guess her excuses, but they are all rubbish because I have never known her be on time for anything. It's the one and only thing that winds me up about her.

Amelia Prescot is very attractive, tall, slim and blonde. Generally my usual type, but not this time. I have an arrangement of sorts with Ami – we help each other out and we've become good friends.

There are a lot of business functions that must be attended, and I pretty much hate the thought of them. It's mainly middle-class balding men going on about their new cars, wives' new tits, which secretary they are banging and their houses in the Riviera. I just can't stand it! But needs must, because 90 percent of all big business transactions are made there. It's still a case of who you know, not what you know, so we attend them together.

Ami is a senior architect at one of the big companies, trying to get partner, and if she has a date with her, the likelihood of being hit on are drastically reduced, so that's my role. I need a date for much the same reason. The women at these events are ruthlessly handsy. Plus, if the men see you with a beautiful woman on your arm, you seem more stable, reliable and less likely to shag their wives.

We have dinner out, usually once a fortnight, to catch up. Ami is a great person to get a woman's point of view, for either business or pleasure. Today Ami is twenty minutes late, and saunters in like its nothing. I stand to greet her with a kiss on the cheek. She looks likes she has come straight from work in a navy shift dress and matching blazer, with her hair tied up. "Nice of you to join me... Eventually!" I quip.

"I was at work, you know how it goes."

"What are you drinking? Wine?"

"May as well!" She looks at me quizzically. "You look different!"

"Like how?"

"Not sure. Like happy... Those wrinkles you usually have between your eyes are gone."

"I don't have bloody wrinkles."

"You seem..." She squints at me. "You've met someone!" Her eyes widen as if she's struck gold.

"What? You can tell that by frown lines?" I touch my forehead to find out what she's talking about.

"Wrinkles! And yes. Go on then, deny it!"

I blow out air, resigned to the fact that she can see right through me. "Can we order first?" She looks at her menu and gives a little giggle. The waiter comes over and takes our order. I don't know why she even looks at the menu because she orders the same thing every time we come here.

When the waiter has gone and our drinks have arrived, I wait for the interrogation. "So spill! We missed our last catch-up session and I think I may now know why."

"YOU bailed on me!" I exclaim.

"Whatever! I'm waiting!"

I take a deep breath and start to fill her in on the events of the past month. She looks at me as if she's waiting for some kind of revelation.

"Right so I have the chronology of it all. What I'm missing are how you feel about the whole thing."

That part is a bit harder to put my finger on.

"I don't know. I really like her. She's smart and sexy and really easy to be with. I want to be around her, like, all the time. I'm constantly thinking about her, I have a permanent erection." I think for a minute. "But it's... complicated."

"Complicated? Well if you are talking this way and it's complicated there must be something in it. You usually steer clear of drama or complications."

"But this is really complicated. She has kids, teenagers, and a knobhead ex."

"Wow!"

"AND she's from England!"

"Nothing wrong with that! So am I."

"I know, but I mean she lives in England, so not just around the corner. It can't be casual. Everything has to be planned."

"And what does she think of you?"

"What's not to love? I'm amazing!" I tease, giving her a wide grin which hides the fact that I really don't know how she feels.

"Obviously! But..."

"But what?"

"What does she want from you?"

We are interrupted by the waiter bringing our meals and passing pleasantries. We taste our food, giving me some time to think about what Ami asked.

"I don't know, she has no agenda. The great thing is she doesn't ask for anything, not even attention. But..." I think about Emma for a moment with a smile on my face. "But... She seems like she's been hiding herself for a while and I see glimpses of the real her, then something will happen and she hides it away again. But in all honesty, I feel like a love-sick teenager, I've gone totally crazy. Sean is taking the piss out of me at work for being distracted over a woman."

"You've got it bad. I've never seen you like this before."

"You have no idea. I want to do things just to get her attention. I would do absolutely anything she wanted."

"What about your little hareem of fuck buddies?"

"Dunno. I've not seen any of them since I met her. I've been avoiding them. The only one to really notice is Tiff."

"Which one is that?"

"You know, the one who went to St. Andrews." I continue when she looks blankly at me. "Daddy has a yacht."

"Nope, no clue!"

"Anyway, I'm gonna have to tell her straight. Even if nothing comes from me and Emma, I'm not going back there, she's just too needy, plus I don't even think she's interested in me for me. That's the difference between the two of them. It's hard to explain." I think for a minute then continue. "If I was Ben the builder, Tiff wouldn't even give me a second of her time, but I don't think anything would be different for Emma."

"That *is* something!" She has a massive smile on her face. At least one of my friends is happy for me.

"You know I sent Emma flowers last week and had to check my phone every few minutes for a text to say she had received them. Who have I actually become?" I hold my head in my hands.

"Well I'm really pleased for you. You deserve someone like that. What do the boys think?"

"Well Sean knows everything, and apart from taking the piss he is happy because I'm not an arsehole at work when I've seen her. The others, I'm not sure. I have a feeling Piers speaks to the other girls. He hasn't said it, but he knows what's going on without me saying."

"Piers is very observant. He acts like the joker, but he's a lot deeper."

"Anyway, enough about me. What about you? Anyone on your radar?"

"Not really. A few hook ups, but nothing special." But there's a look in her eye that means there is something going on. I'll just need to see how that develops because Amelia is special and I don't want to see her get hurt.

We finish our meals and Ami pays the bill – we alternate who buys dinner. We leave and say our goodbyes as I make sure she gets into her car and leaves the carpark. I get in my car and have to stop myself from ringing Emma. I think she'll run a mile if she knows just how into her I am. Instead I decide to make the call to Tiff. May as well get this over and done with.

Chapter Thirteen

I'm sitting at my desk and Sean walks through the door.

"Mate, I have something I need to you look at. I know it's last minute but it could be just what we are looking for. I've just emailed you the link."

I look back at my laptop and open my inbox, click on the link he has sent through for an auction.

"This is for tonight?"

"Yes I know, but look at lot 18." There's something in his voice that makes it seem important.

I scroll through the information on the properties and find the relevant one.

"Shit! That's what we were talking about with Joel. But it's tonight, just outside Newcastle."

"I know," he says. "It's a bit of a drive and I can't go, I have to meet with some potential investors tonight. I was hoping you could come as well, but I think this takes precedence. And we definitely need to be at this in person to get a feel for who is on the lookout."

I nod in agreement. "Right! If I head off now, I'll have about an hour to spare. I'll see if there are any rooms at the hotel its being held at."

"You have a breakfast meeting tomorrow that you can't miss. Sorry, I know it's a bit much, but it would be a shame to miss out."

"I'll have to go now and drive back straight afterwards." I start to pack up my laptop and grab my jacket before heading for the door. "Can you request a copy of the legal pack for that property and email it onto me? I'll read it once I'm there."

"No problem!" Sean replies and heads into his own office.

I grab my phone from my pocket and dial. I think it's going to answer machine when she answers in her light tone. "Hi Ben, everything ok?"

"Yes! I just wanted to hear your beautiful voice." I think that flattery might butter her up a bit, but in all honesty, I love hearing her, I love talking to her but most of all I love seeing her, so I had a bit of a plan. She blows out a breath as if she doesn't believe me, I know she just rolled her eyes. "Actually, I know it's really short notice, AND it's a bit of an ask AND I totally understand if you can't..." Although I will be gutted if she can't.

"Spit it out Ben!"

"I've just got a last-minute auction at the racecourse in New-castle this evening. I'm heading there now. I can't stay over because I have a breakfast meeting in the morning. I thought, because it was in your vicinity, we could maybe see each other." There is a pause on the other end and I realise what I've said is pretty ridiculous and start to back track. "Sorry it was a stupid idea, I'm only gonna be there for an hour or so, I shouldn't have asked."

She blows out a breath. "What were you thinking, coming here for a bit?"

"I won't get to yours and back to the auction in time. I was hoping you would meet me there." I pause again. "Sorry! It's a bit much to ask. I was being selfish."

"It's about a 40 minute drive for me to get there," she says, leaving another long pause.

"I know, just forget it. Like I say, I've just found out about it."

"What time will you get there?" she asks and hope ignites in my chest.

"I'll get there about 5, auction starts at 6."

"I don't know. Can you leave it with me?"

"Of course, I'm getting in my car now."

"I'll send you a text to let you know." Well it's not an outright no. And Emma is honest. If she wasn't prepared to try, she would have just said no. "Drive safely," she finishes.

"I will... Bye!" I hang up quickly. Jesus Christ, I just had to stop myself from saying *love you* to end the call. What the hell has got into me? I think she has me under some kind of spell.

I stopped for petrol as I got nearer the venue and checked my phone to find a message saying Emma would meet me there. I haven't stopped smiling since. I am sitting in the seating area of the hotel lobby, reading the legal documents Sean sent through, some notes he made about it and our ceiling offer.

Something catches my eye and I look up. There she is coming through the door. She hasn't seen me yet, which is great because it means I can spend a few moments just taking her in. And fuck, she looks amazing. She must have come straight from work in her tight pencil skirt and cream blouse with a ruffle over her chest. The sun is shining behind her so I can see her outline through the slightly see-through top. Her hair is up and she has some big round thick rimmed glasses that I've never seen before. She looks amazingly fuckable! She sees me and a smile spreads across her face as she heads in my direction. I stand to greet her.

"Ms Lowther!".

"Mr Ambrose," she answers with a smirk.

"You look like every male manager's wet dream! Gorgeous!"

She laughs, "And every HR's nightmare!"

"This is why I don't have a PA." I look her up and down.

"Well I can fill that role if you're looking?" she says with a flirty look. We take a seat and I just can't stop smiling at her.

"What's the plan?" she asks, and I answer with a strange look, because I honestly can't think further than trying to get her clothes off. "The auction? Are you buying something?"

"Oh yeah. There's something Sean found. It fits the bill for a project we have in the pipeline."

"Okay. I've never been to an auction before, can I stay? I'd like to see the CEO at work."

"I'd love you to. Do you want a drink or something to eat? The auction starts in about 45 minutes."

"Coffee would be great. I didn't sleep well. Hence the glasses." She points at her face. "I need them if I'm tired, mainly. And maybe something quick to eat."

"What kept you up?"

She shrugs "Just my normal overthinking brain. It doesn't have to be anything. I just can't get random stuff out of my head. I'll go over conversations I've had two years ago and think of the things I should have said." I laugh. She is adorable. But there's a pause and she turns serious. "And I have been thinking more about the shitty situation with David."

"And have you come up with any solutions?" I ask, hoping she has found a way to stop that prick having so much power over her.

"I never said my thoughts were constructive."

"I'm not going to give you my opinion because I don't think you'd appreciate me having one. Just that you deserve someone who only thinks about you and your needs."

"And are you suggesting that that person maybe you, Mr Ambrose?" she says with one eyebrow raised, teasing me.

"Absolutely not. I'm a selfish bastard and only think about getting your clothes off," I say. Which is mainly a lie. But I do want to get her alone, so I can at least kiss her properly. I can't get my mind onto anything else, which isn't a good plan if I'm going to be bidding in an auction. "Shall we head into the bar to get something?" She nods and we both stand up to make our way through.

We walk down the corridor towards the bar. Seeing an opportunity, I spy a door with the sign 'store room'. I try the door and find it unlocked. I grab her and pull her inside with me. She squeals as I push her up against a shelf stacked with table linen. I close and lock the door behind us.

"What are you doing?" she asks, slightly shocked at my sudden actions.

"I just wanted a little alone time, and we haven't got long." Before she can answer my lips are on her and I'm teasing open her mouth with mine. Eventually her body relaxes, her arms go round my neck and she kisses me back. But it's not enough. I need more, I need her. I turn her round and walk her back a few steps until she hits a set of drawers. I push her tight skirt up her legs to gain access, revealing stockings underneath.

"Fuck! You're wearing stockings?"

"Yes, I had a ladder in the last of my tights," she explains.

"If that's the reason for wearing them, I'm gonna put a ladder in every last pair!"

I kiss her again. I'm so hard. All the blood has rushed to my dick and all I can think about is being inside her. In one fluid movement I've lifted her up on top of the drawers and wrapped her legs round my waist. I'm not sure how far she'll let this go but I just need to be closer. As if she's having the same thoughts her hand moves towards my waistband, opens the zipper and slips inside, wrapping her hand around me. I let out a moan that sounds more of a growl as she moves her hand.

"This is gonna get very messy if you keep doing that." I say into her ear.

Her breath hitches and she stills her hand and whispers, "You better do something about it then!"

I pull away from her and take a condom out of my pocket. In the quickest time ever, I put it on, move her pants to one side and slip myself inside her. We stay still. All I can hear is our breath as we both pant, Emma acclimatising to my invasion.

I move my hand up the delicate fabric of her blouse and over her breasts. I can feel her hard peaks and she groans as I brush over them.

"This is going to be over very quickly if you keep making those noises." Her laugh turns to a moan when I start to move inside her. But it's true. All my nerve endings are on a massive assault and I can feel my orgasm growing. I need to stop it. I need to think of anything but her, here, right now. I think about the spreadsheet that I can never quite get to make sense to give myself a bit more time.

I put my hands underneath her arse and pull her forward, tilting my angle and she lets out a moan and starts panting. I love that I have her all worked up and look at the expression on her face. She's flushed and looks absolutely stunning. I start to move again, thrusting into her with my hips. I'm totally lost in the woman. The way she feels around me, the way she can't get enough of me. The thought has me moving at a piston pace. Then I feel her tense before she explodes and starts to shake. She contracts and pulses all around me and it's just the best feeling in the world. A feeling that pushes me over the edge.

As our pulses die down I learn forwards and take a long kiss, then pull away to rest my forehead with hers.

"I did warn you it would be quick!"

She laughs but isn't able to form words yet. I slide out of her and discard the condom, then I take the opportunity to steal more kisses.

"Well that's another first for me," she says. I look at her blankly and she gets the hint to elaborate. "Quicky sex in a store cupboard. I think you are corrupting me, Mr Ambrose." I tuck myself in and zip up, then help her down.

"Glad to be of service. I wonder if there are any more firsts I can cross off the list?"

"We'll see," she says, straightening her skirt as I open the door a crack to see if the coast is clear. When it is safe to come out, we slip out and head to the bar to find a seat.

We order some light bites and coffee and chat about work until it's time to go into the auction room. The room is the usual set up. Rows of seats in front of a podium with a display screen. We find some seats near the back because I like to be able to see who I'm bidding against. All evidence of our encounter is gone apart from Emma's flushed face. Now it's back to business. I've taken a quick call from Sean and we are ready to go. I show Emma the property we are looking to purchase.

"It's not what I was expecting," she says. "It's more industrial. It has a gangland killing vibe to it!"

I laugh "Well I hope not! But it's a regeneration that we are hoping to do. If we're really lucky, no one else will have realised its potential." The first few lots go quickly and Emma is looking excited. I whisper in her ear.

"Poker face! If someone sees how much of an interest we have, we'll be in a bidding war. We need to keep the element of surprise, as if we just happened to stumble across it, last minute."

"I have no poker face!" She frowns at me. "If I think it, the words may not come out of my mouth, but my face will say it. I can't switch it off!"

"Good to know..." I laugh. She's just amazing. I focus back on our lot that's just getting started.

After a few hand raises and some discreet nodding, the auctioneer announces, "Sold to number 459!"

"Is that it?" she asks in a surprised voice. I nod. "I expected it to be a lot more dramatic than that."

"Well luckily for us, no one was really that interested, so it didn't even hit our ceiling bid." She looks disappointed. "That's a good thing!"

"If you say so! What now then?"

"I just have to sort some paperwork and that's it really."

"So you came all the way down here for five minutes? Couldn't you have just done a phone bid or something?"

"Well I like to see who else is here. It gauges whether there will be any fall out or issues." I look at her for a few moments and take in her features. "And if I didn't, I wouldn't have seen you, would I?"

She looks back at me. "But I was only a side note to your main event!"

"Emma, you'll always be my main event!" I look at her and try to keep what I said light.

"Always the charmer!" She gives me a smile but I don't smile back, I'm deadly serious. She thinks that I'm just being flirty but it's 100 percent true. This woman is starting to be my everything and she doesn't even realise it.

"Come on, let's get this sorted," I say, standing up and taking her hand. She looks at me like she is working out what 'this' means. "The paperwork!"

"Oh right, yes. Then I'm going to have to head back. I've left the boys to order take out and at least try not to kill each other."

I sort the paperwork out quickly and message Sean the good news. Then we head out to our cars. Emma has parked next to me. "I just parked next to the flashiest car I could find," she laughs.

"So when will we see each other again?" I bring the conversation back to reality. I lean against my car, hands in my pockets, trying to seem casual when I am actually desperate. If I don't have a plan of when I'll see her next, I'll not be able to focus. My phone begins to ring in my pocket and I take it out, glance at the screen and Ami's name flash up. I kill the call and put it back in my pocket, she'll understand.

"Anyone important?"

"Clearly not! Stop changing the subject." I'm getting a little impatient.

"It was you that was distracted," she says with an annoyed undertone.

"Now I'm not." I take a deep breath and repeat the question. "So when will we get to see each other again?"

"I don't know. Things aren't that easy for me." Her expression is pained.

"I get that," I say, and then my needy side starts to appear and I blow out a breath. "Do you even want this?" I gesture between us and I instantly regret it.

Her barriers have gone up and she bites back. "I'm here aren't I?" She folds her arms across her chest and glares at me. "I dropped everything, left work early, sorted my kids, drove nearly 30 miles in school run traffic, which if you don't realise, is actual hell on earth, just to spend an hour with you." She pauses to compose herself. "So yes, I do even want this." She copies my gesture, "whatever THIS is!"

"I'm sorry!" I say, after giving the situation time to settle. "If I had the option, I would want to spend every day with you. I know that's not possible, but that's how much I want this." I look at her to gauge her reaction. "Like I said, I'm selfish!"

"And I would love to be selfish… but I can't." There is tension in the air that I never wanted. I didn't mean to push her so much.

A few moments pass before I continue. "Have a think about our next meet up. But please don't let us leave each other like this." I lean off the car and move towards her, wrapping my arms around her and pulling her in for a hug. I feel her relax a little in my arms and I know it will be ok. I pull away slightly, "Can we say our goodbye now?" She nods and I curl my hand around her neck and kiss her lips. I move my tongue into her mouth, possessing her, and she kisses me back with full force. I want her to feel how much she affects me.

Even though I don't want it to end, I break away from her, and plant another quick kiss on her lips. "Bye then!" I want to say something more but it's not the right time.

"Bye then," She repeats back and gets into her car. I walk around the front of mine and get in. I wait until she pulls out and follow her to the exit. She signals left while I signal right, which seems very apt for the situation. She flashes her hazards, I flash my light and we go our separate ways.

Chapter Fourteen

Emma

I have had a few days to think about what happened on Ben's last visit, but I've come to no conclusion. I was cross with him, inferring that I wasn't particularly invested in whatever it is we have going. And it probably looks that way to him I suppose, but I do have other people to consider. I would absolutely love to drop everything to see him, which I pretty much did that day. But life is different for me. I do feel something for him, I think about him constantly. I smile when he sends me a message and when I get a gift in the post.

Am I just making excuses? Can I change things so it's not as complicated or am I just stuck in the situation I have been in the last few years? He has made it clear that he has feelings for me, but can I really be everything he deserves, everything we both deserve? Or am I just blaming the people around me for my situation, rather than pulling myself out of this rut and making a future for myself?

Maybe I need to be a bit more proactive and offer him a bit more of me and see what happens. Maybe he will see I am just plain boring me and give up? My head is all over the place at the minute. I'm sitting at my desk, not really being very productive and I open my diary to see what the next few weeks have to offer. The weekends that David has the boys are written in pencil, because it has a likelihood to change. I flick through the pages and realise that the kids have a school holiday coming up.

I used to get so anxious about school holidays. Having to keep the children fed and occupied, and all the expectations of spending fabulous family time *making memories,* which really consisted of the kids having varying degrees of tantrum and loading them back into the car and swearing under my breath.

Now school holidays are a relief. There are no worries about getting the kids up and out of the door, that school will ring to say to pick them up or that I'll receive a hundred thousand messages vis the four different apps they have to *keep you informed.* Now I just need to have food in the fridge and a working internet connection.

And there it is. As if someone from above has intervened, there are two entries that make my heart jump for joy. Noah, away two nights with school and Josh, camping with Jack. My heart does a little leap. It's practically unheard of that those two have plans made at the same time, and if they do, they usually clash in the opposite directions, pulling me several different ways.

I had completely forgotten about both of these. Noah is going with the school to London, I can't quite remember why. I stopped listening after about ten minutes of Noah's explanation, all I know is it cost a small fortune.

And Josh? Jack's dad – Jack being Joshua's closest friend – decided to take a few of the boys on a Bear Grylls type survival trip, camping in the woods. I warned him that it was all on him. I had no desire to either go with them, or drive into the middle of the night at stupid o'clock to rescue them. So that means two nights, or three days if I ask Lizzie to pick up Noah with her Jacob from the coach, all on my own. How did I ever miss the fact that I had completely child-free days?

This means I can make plans with Ben and do something for myself for a change. It means I don't have everything dependant on what kind of mood David is in. I think maybe this needs to be a conversation with Ben rather than a message. I start to feel all excited. I've tried not to get myself all worked up about him because, in all honesty, I'm waiting for the other shoe to drop, and for him to say, 'actually Emma I can't be arsed with your shit' or something. I pick up my phone and walk out of the office to ring him.

It rings a few times. I think it's going to go to answer machine and the doubt starts to kick in. Maybe he is screening my calls. We've not spoken that much since the auction. Maybe he's having second thoughts. But just as I'm about to hang up, not wanting to leave a message, he answers.

"Hey Princess." Relief floods over me.

"Hey, can you talk?"

"Erm, yes." He sounds a bit apprehensive. "I have about ten minutes before I go into a meeting. What's up?"

"So…" I have a nervous excitement about telling him. "I have just looked through my diary."

"And?"

"And…. I seem to have three days… ish… with no kids." I pause, waiting for some kind of reaction. But there is none. "And maybe we could do something?" I pause again, waiting for him to give me some kind of indication of what he is thinking.

"Okay!" He draws out as if he's waiting for the catch, which of course, with me, there always is. But now I'm wondering if I got it all wrong, and if he really doesn't want to spend the time with me.

"But it's midweek!" There's still nothing his end and I can't really deal with the torture. "If you have too much on at work, I'll totally understand." But would also be absolutely devasted but I'm not going to tell him that.

"I'm sure I could work something out. What were you thinking and when is it?"

"It's the week after next and I have no thoughts. I've only just realised, and I didn't want to think any further in case you said no."

"Why would I ever say no to spending time with you?"

"I don't know, I just couldn't gauge your reaction, you didn't say much!" He laughs but I'm not sure why.

"Well now I've said yes, do you have any thoughts?"

"I thought… I would leave it up to you."

"So do you want to go away? Stay at home? Can you give me some indication at least?"

"I definitely don't want to stay at mine, there's potential for disaster. Other than that, I really don't mind. But I hate surprises. It's totally up to you what we do, but I need to know about it before we go. I like to be prepared."

"That sounds fair." He thinks for a few moments. "I really do have to go to this meeting now, but if you send me the days, what time you can leave and what time you need to be back for, I'll have a think and plan something."

"Okay then…" I hang on the little a bit longer. "Ben! Thank you."

"What for? You don't know what we're doing yet, you may hate it!"

"I doubt it. Bye!"

"Bye Princess."

Chapter Fifteen

Ben

What an unexpected call from Emma. I wasn't sure what was going on in her head since we left each other after the auction. She was mad with me, hell I was mad with me. I had pushed her too far to get a bit of attention, but it had backfired.

When she called, I thought she was going to end it. She sounded all serious. When she mentioned the kids being away and having two nights we could spend together, I punched the air and got a bit carried away with the joy I didn't answer her and she thought I was trying to turn her down, which was exactly my opposite plan.

I had to go straight to a meeting after that and I couldn't wipe the smile off my face. Sean was very suspicious, especially when I announced that I had to take a few days off. I NEVER take time off, so it came as a surprise. But I think he will be happy to be rid of my rollercoaster of moods. I can't keep up with them myself. I

keep beating myself up about possibly blowing everything with
Emma, and then at the tiniest bit of contact she gives me, I'm
like the happiest man alive.

Emma messaged me the dates and times, so I need to get planning. I dropped Ami a message asking for ideas, but I already
had a plan forming. Emma doesn't want a surprise, but I really
want to make it special. So, I drop her a message.

**Me: I promise I will tell you where we are going nearer
the time. But I want you to guess too x**

Emma: Sounds intriguing!

Me: Also, If I'm deciding, then it's on me, no arguments.

Emma: But

Me: No arguments, my treat!

Emma: Okay

I go back to my internet search. I need something extra special
but not too flashy. Something romantic but not contrived. Most
of all I want something where we can just be us, together, where
we can both get a taste of what it could be like being together.
Where she can be the fun, relaxed Emma that I adore. Somewhere we can be a couple. Do couple things, hold hands, go for
meal and obviously have lots and lots of sex.

My phone vibrates and I see a message from Ami.

Ami: Don't do anything stupid?

Me: I don't know what you mean!

Ami: Don't scare her away, be subtle!

Me: I'm always subtle

Ami: *rolling eyes emoji*

She doesn't know what she's talking about!

Chapter Sixteen

Emma

I'm all kinds of excited for our time together, but I have no idea where we are going. Ben insisted on booking and paying for everything, which is a sure-fire way of it being expensive and over the top. He knows I don't care about money, but treating me, whether its sending flowers or taking me to nice places, is Ben's love language.

But I absolutely hate surprises. I don't like being out of control. I need a plan. I need to know what time I need to be somewhere and whether I need to pack for the beach or for the mountains. Ben has insisted that he sends me clues, but he will reveal the whole plan before we go, which fits into his love of surprises and my hate of them.

What Ben doesn't realise is that I'm really good at guessing games. My parents always got frustrated by the fact we could name our Christmas presents, just from a feel through the wrapping. One year, as a joke, my mum wrapped a roll of dish-cloths to throw us off the scent, but I knew straight away, just by the feel. I'm like a detective when it comes to the challenge, but I don't want to spoil his little game.

The first clue he sent me was a bouquet of irises and lilies, which I know are the national flowers of France. Well I didn't know exactly that, but I had an inkling that was what they would represent, so I Googled which country. I deduced it could be the South of France, but for a few days' stay it wouldn't justify the journey. It could also be a Gite in the Normandy countryside, but as Ben is a big city slicker, I suspected it to be two nights in Paris. When he asked, I didn't give the game away because he's so excited. And they were beautiful flowers. I was, again, the envy of the office.

The second clue came through the post a few days later, to the house. It was a postcard with a picture of a chicken on. So that confirms it is definitely France, although technically it should have been a picture of a cockerel. I send him a quick message to tell him I received it.

Me: Thanks for the postcard. I hope this doesn't mean we are staying on a farm cos I can't stand chickens...

Me: Unless it's in a restaurant and I'm eating it.

Ben: Actually I couldn't find a large cock, it's more a clue to what you'll be getting, rather than where we are heading.

Me: Very funny.

Always the joker, that man. I appreciated the sentiment. I usually only get bills through the post. Everything is so instant now, but I love the thought of a letter or a postcard.

The next clue I received was to work again, about which my colleagues were equally perplexed and happy. A selection of French patisserie goodies. There was a massive white cardboard box delivered, full to the brim of croissants, pain au chocolat, choux buns and all kinds of pastries that I had never seen before. They were delicious. I obviously Googled the place he sent them from and they were not cheap.

I messaged him and asked if he was just trying to sweeten me up for the trip, or make me fat so I don't fit into any of my clothes. But I still didn't give away that I had worked out where we were going.

The fourth and fifth clue came in quick succession. The fourth was a DVD of Les Miserable, and the fifth, though not a clue, was our flight tickets with Air France, from Newcastle to Charles De Gaulle airport.

I pick my phone up to call him. It only rings once before he answers. "Hi Princess, did you get my latest offerings?"

"I did indeed. We're going to Paris?"

"Yes!" He sounds pleased with himself but then second guesses and his voice drops. "Is that okay? We could go somewhere else if you don't like the sound of that?"

"It's a really lovely idea."

"You think it's too much?" I kind of do, but I think that's mainly because I had been wanting David to take me for years and he consistently put it off. I have been seeing Ben five minutes and this is what he has organised.

"No! Well maybe, but I have always wanted a romantic trip to Paris."

"When did you work it out?"

"Honestly?" I pause, not knowing whether I should tell the truth. "From the flowers!"

"What? I thought that was subtle."

"What you hadn't bargained on was that I am, in fact, a super detective." I laugh.

"I can change it to somewhere less romantic if you like?" I feel really guilty. "Amsterdam maybe?"

"No! I love that you want to take me to Paris. I've always wanted to go. To walk along the Seine, catch the Eifel Tower at night and maybe see the Mona Lisa in the Louvre!"

"Or we could spend the whole time in the hotel room?"

"Then we may as well just stay here!"

"I would do anything, just to spend some time with you." I can tell he really means it, but he also enjoys spoiling me too, doing things I wouldn't usually have the chance to. He really is something else.

Chapter Seventeen

Ben has driven down from Edinburgh to collect me and take us to the airport. We travel in almost silence. There is a bit of an uneasiness about Ben today. I'm not sure what is on his mind. We check our bags and mill about the airport for a bit before we board our flight. Once we are on board and ready for take-off, Ben turns to me with a serious expression.

"I can see how you may have thought this trip was a bit much, but let me take you through my thought process."

"You really don't have to, it was a lovely idea." He has obviously been stewing about this.

"Humour me!" he says, and I nod for him to continue. "So I wanted us to get away, somewhere that is far enough for us to escape and not too far that we just spend all our time travelling. I wanted somewhere we could be out and about together, as a couple, doing things. So it had to be a city." He has a point, all our meet ups have been pretty much in our own little bubble that it didn't really seem real. "I didn't pick Paris to show you my romantic side. Although now I come to think of it, that works for me too."

"I wasn't unhappy about you choosing Paris, you've got me all wrong, although it did cross my mind that it wasn't a very third date kinda trip." He shrugs but I continue. "It was more that I was sad, that after all those years of David promising to take me, he never bothered. And for you, it was an obvious choice, even without knowing my eagerness to visit."

"Are you sad that it isn't David taking you?"

"Hell no. I'm sad I spent so much time with a man who didn't want to do things with me, just because I might like them. We were always on his timetable, his agenda."

"I actually didn't know you wanted to go and in all honesty I'm glad you didn't go with David, because he didn't deserve it and it means all your memories of Paris are with me."

"So let's just leave all that behind and enjoy it!"

"Sounds good. We'll head straight to the hotel, drop our things and do some exploring."

We get a taxi from the airport and I stare out of the window at the bustling city, in awe of the grandeur of the buildings. We pull up outside a grand, stone and glass building that looks out over the river. There is a doorman who gets our bags from the taxi while Ben helps me out of the car. I stand on the pavement looking up at the opulent architecture in front of me. "This is where we are staying?"

"Yes. Do you like it?"

"Wow!" Is all I can muster.

This isn't only the smartest hotel I've ever stayed at, it's the smartest hotel I've ever seen. We walk into the entrance hall and I'm well aware of how out of place I look. My eyes are immediately drawn to the ceiling with its Sistine Chapel-style décor and the chandelier, with what seems like hundreds of tiny light bulbs.

Ben takes my hand and steers me towards the reception. But before we get there, a very well-dressed man approaches Ben.

"Mr and Mrs Ambrose, how lovely it is for you to be joining us here at the Hotel Du Pont." His French accent is soft and sing-songy. I raise my eyebrows to Ben at the Mrs Ambrose comment, but he doesn't correct him.

"Thank you!" He looks to me with a cheeky smile.

"I will take you up to your suite." He ushers us into the lift and presses the button for the fourth floor. I look at Ben with wide eyes and he just returns a sly grin as the concierge talks us through breakfast times or whatever, I'm not really listening. I feel a bit underdressed for this place, but that seems to be the normal predicament when I'm with Ben. I expect the rest of the female guests are dressed in high-end floaty dresses and designer sunglasses, whereas I'm in my jeans, an oversized jumper and tatty pumps. At least I'll be comfortable, I tell myself.

The lift stops and the doors open. We follow him along a corridor which could have been modelled on the palace of Versailles. We get to a door and he unlocks it with the key card and walks in. The place is amazing, with a mix with old French features and new modern glass. The whole of the outside wall is windows that look over the river – a breath-taking view. The living area flows through to a bedroom and bathroom that is marble and glass partitions.

I go back to look out of the windows, totally mesmerised by the view. I feel him come up behind me. The concierge has left, and Ben wraps him arms around me and pulls my back flush with his chest.

"This must have cost a fortune", I say.

"Well that's not something you need to think about. Plus you aren't interested in money." Which is totally true. Money, or the lack of it, doesn't change who you are as a person.

"True, but don't think I have forgotten the Mrs Ambrose thing." He laughs and starts trailing kisses down my neck. "So what's first?"

"Well, let's get you naked and start from there."

"I thought we were going out, to explore?"

"Well I won't be able to enjoy the scenery if all I can think about is getting you naked."

"One track mind!"

"Yes, and that track is called 'Emma'!"

He turns me to face him. But instead of leaning down to kiss me, he ducks down further, grabs my thighs and lifts me like a fireman. He carries me over to the bed. He drops me and I bounce slightly, letting out a giggle. "Now, let's get you out of these clothes." He stands at the end of the bed and pulls off my pumps, then crawls up the bed, over the top of me, with a mischievous grin on his face.

I'm caged, his taut arms either side of my shoulders. Leaning down, he plants a kiss on my lips before scooting down to unbutton my jeans. "These need to come off!" I love this playful side of him. As he opens my jeans and wriggles them down my hips, he leaves a trail of kisses, the last one hitting that sweet spot. Then he jumps up and grabs the bottom of the legs and tries to pull them off, only to mainly take me with them with a squeal.

Eventually the jeans are off, knickers have come with them and he throws them on the floor. The jumper comes off next, followed by the vest top and bra. Ben stands over me with a wide smile.

"Are you just gonna stand over me, or are you gonna take some clothes off?" My question seems to pull him out of his trace. With a rush, he takes off his clothes, which is a shame because it means less time appreciating his amazing body. I just want to lick all the way down his abs. Slowly he stalks his way back up the bed and makes his way up my body, coming to rest facing me, his whole weight resting on his taut forearms.

He angles his head to plant another kiss, then goes back for more, running his tongue along my lips to encourage me to open up. When I do he devours me, taking my breath away. When we come up for air, he gives me that look, the one as if he's wondering if we are both really there. "I love being here with you."

"I love being here with you," I reply

"Well then open up and let me in," he says, taking an arm away and tapping me on the thigh. I do as I'm told, and he nudges himself inside me. We both moan at the feeling. It's not rushed, it's not feverish, it's slow, sensual and the pleasure builds with each movement.

I think I'm falling for this guy and I'm not sure if I can stop it. Or even if I want to. I just know this is the best feeling,

having him here, just focused on me. For the first time he's the
only thing in my thoughts, everything else pushed out because
there's no room. There's just us.

We eventually head out and hit the street to do some exploring.
I feel nice and relaxed, ready for anything. The concierge has
given us some pointers – the usual tourist things and a few off
track. We walk along the banks of the Seine hand in hand and it
feels strange, unfamiliar but nice. We've never had this kind of
freedom before and I'm really enjoying it. It feels just so natural
with this man. We chat about everything and nothing.

We walk through the Parisian streets, in no particular direction, with no place to be, which is something I'm not used to,
but I'm loving it. Ben has not broken contact with me the whole
time. He only dropped my hand to wrap his arm round me to
take a photo. And when he needed two hands to pay and take
our yummy goodies in a gorgeous patisserie, he took my hand
and hooked it into his back pocket.

We have walked around for hours and its starting to get dark,
we head to the Eifel Tower to see it lit up in all its glory. It's a
scene you usually see on postcards or on your Instagram feed.
We walk around the park to gain our best vantage spot. Once
we get it, we stand back to take full advantage of the scene. Ben
wraps me in his arms.

"Is that what you wanted to see?"

I look up at the hundreds of lights illuminating the iron
structure and nod. I can't believe where I am and who I'm with.

There's an enormous amount of emotion I'm feeling, I can't quite explain all of them. Ben turns me round so I'm looking up into his eyes, and threads his hand under my hair and around my neck. He presses his lips to mine. I melt into him as he swipes his tongue over my lips and I open up to him. Our whole surroundings slip away as nothing else matters other than being with each other.

We eventually pull away and he takes his phone out of his pocket. "This needs to be documented!" He smiles as we pose for a photo, then we turn towards each other and kiss again, I hear another photo being taken. He looks at the photos and goes to share them.

"Where are you sending them?" I ask in a panic.

"Just to you. This is nobody's business but ours." It's true and I don't want anyone to break this little romance we have with their questions and opinions.

Once we've had our fill of the moment, we head towards the restaurant that was recommended by the concierge. We walk through the door and Ben speaks to the waiter in perfect French, which is a surprise as it's the first time this trip and I didn't even know he spoke French.

We are seated in a private little corner at the back. Ben orders for us. This place is the kind that doesn't really tolerate tourists and refuses to converse in anything other than French and distain. Once we have our drinks, Ben looks at me with his serious face and I know that this is going to be a conversation about the future. "So what are your thoughts about this, about us?" I was right. I look at him for a minute and frown. I'm not really sure what my feelings are, they're all a muddle of practicalities and lust. As if reading my mind he continues, "They don't have to be fully formed thoughts, maybe just the gist."

"About this trip or in general?" I ask.

"Let's start with the trip and go from there."

"Well I'm really enjoying being here, being with you. I haven't once thought about work or all the things I have to do when I get back."

"That's good!" He looks content with my answer.

"I've thought about the boys but only in the, *I bet they're having a great time*, kind of way." He gives me one of his winning smiles. "It's nice to live in the moment for once. I don't need to think about anyone else's issues, I don't have to manage anyone, I just have to...BE!"

"I'm just loving being with you. You know, the unguarded Emma, like the drunk one from the club? It is really lovely to see." I laugh because he's right.

"But I can't be that Emma back home, which is sad. I know you want a piece of me, and I want to give you one, but I'm not sure how big a piece I can give you." The mood has changed, and the reality of life back home is making me uneasy.

"I know." He looks sad. "Like I said, I'm selfish and I like being with you."

"I like you, a LOT. And although you'll have to share my time, I want you all to myself. I'm selfish too."

"Being a bit possessive Ms Lowther?"

"Absolutely. But I thought I was Mrs Ambrose here? I'm actually quite surprised you didn't have some kind of seizure when he said that."

"Why would I be unhappy at the assumption you were my wife?" He has a puzzled look on his face.

"I don't know." The waiter brings out our meals and we thank him. "Who else gets mistaken for your wife?" It's not particularly subtle way of asking if he has other women lined up.

"Is this you trying to ascertain if there are others?" He looks at me quizzically, but the curl of a smile at the corner of his mouth gives him away.

"Maybe... Actually no, don't answer that, I don't want to know." I think I'm happy in ignorant bliss.

"Well you'll be happy to know there is no other Mrs Ambrose." I am happy with that. "I may have had a bit of a reputation, way back in the past, but there hasn't been anyone else since you." I'm not sure I want to know of his reputation, because the 'why me' doubts will start to kick in.

"No one since the hotel?" I ask.

"No one since I first laid eyes on you in that bar!"

"I'm not sure I believe you. You are such a smooth talker." I smile at him. "Plus, your phone never stops. I bet you'll tell me that's all work." It has been playing on my mind, the number of messages he receives constantly. It can't all be from Sean about business. Sean knows he's having time off and wouldn't keep interrupting with work. But seeing Ami's name flash up a few times puts me a bit on edge.

"It is business, mainly! I have retired my little black book." He laughs and then looks serious again before starting the interrogation back up. "So... After? What are your thoughts on that, how do you see it working?"

I pause trying to get my words right, but the talk of other women is making me feel on edge. "I mean, do you want it to work?" It comes out a bit too harsh.

"If you don't know by now that I want this, then I'm definitely doing something wrong!"

"Okay that came out wrong. It's just I don't know what you want from me." I give a sigh and continue. "To be honest, I don't know what I want either." He's really made me start thinking about what I want in life. "I feel like I am just trudging through life, dealing with other people's stuff."

"You know you don't have to do that alone."

"Maybe, but I don't know how to do *together* either. You know? How do all the components of my life merge together, without conflict?"

"Maybe some conflict is needed to make change."

"I know, I just hate the thought of it."

"So in an ideal world. Where everyone is happily joined together, where would you have us?"

"I don't know. Together?"

"Together! Well that's a start."

"As we don't have that ideal world, I haven't really thought it through. I love spending time together, but I'm not sure whether, with the amount of planning involved, moving things around and compromise needed, you'll come to resent me."

"Why would I resent you?"

"It's more the resenting me being unable to drop everything to be with each other. Or will this end up as nothing more than just quick hook ups?" I sigh. "Don't get me wrong, the sex is great, but I'll want more, you'll want more and what if I can't give you that?"

"But what if it does all work out?" He looks at me with a pained expression. "Can we just see how it goes?" He's forever the optimist.

"Yes of course. I just need to know we are on the same page, or at least reading the same book." He sighs and I think I have deflated the mood. It wasn't my intention. "Let's just enjoy our time together. We'll not think about the *what next* part!" We carry on our meal in relative silence. The words swirling around both of us and I regret what I said. I regret the negative way I came about things, but that's just how my brain works, I'm a realist.

Ben pays the bill and we head for the door. "Where now?" he asks and I'm wondering whether he means metaphorically or physically.

"We've done lots of walking, how about we head back and have a drink in the bar of the hotel," I suggest.

"Okay." His tone betrays the distance that he is feeling.

"I'm sorry!"

"What for?" He looks at me quizzically.

"For all that!" I point back to the restaurant. "For the negative talk. I'm just trying to process everything the only way I know, and I'm sorry if I made you feel..." I try to get the right words without putting my foot in it again. "I don't know.... Like I don't care."

"So you do care? About me?"

"Yes, of course I do," I say looking up at him. There's a wicked grin forming on his face.

He grabs my hand, "Well I care about you too Ms Lowther." He takes my hand and we walk back towards the hotel.

Chapter Eighteen

Ben

I open my eyes and she's there. It's the best feeling in the world waking up next to her. I try not to move so I don't disturb her. She looks so beautiful and relaxed, I just want to take in the view for as long as possible. Her eyes flutter in her sleep and I hold my breath, wondering if she'll wake and find me staring at her.

Although there was the tough conversation yesterday about the future, she also admitted that she had feelings for me. I never thought she would. Sometimes she's so closed off with her feelings towards me, but yesterday hearing her say it made my heart leap. I'm totally and completely falling for this woman, and I know she still has reservations about how it can all work. She thinks I will come to resent her, but in all honesty, I want every minute she is able to offer, without complaint. I just love being around her.

She's lying on her back, her head turned towards me. I chance a gentle kiss to her temple. I just can't resist but hope it's gentle enough not to wake her. I can smell the raspberry of the shampoo in her hair and the slight honey smell from her soap. She must have been exhausted with all that walking around Paris hand in hand, and then back to the hotel to have sex until the early hours. Each time we get close, I see her confidence grow. She now knows what she wants and is willing to take it, with only the smallest direction from me. My only demand was that she was positioned in a way that I could always see her face. How she looked when she came apart has me hard just remembering.

She starts to stir. Her eyes flicker open and she blinks, trying to focus.

"Morning..."

She gives a full arm and body stretch before replying. "Morning! How long have you been staring at me?"

"Not long," I lie, and plant a quick kiss on her lips.

"What's the plan for today then?"

"We could just pick up where we left off. You're already naked so that cuts out that part." I grin down at her.

"We can't stay in bed all day."

"Can't we?"

"Not when we have the whole of Paris out there." She points to the window.

"What did you have in mind?"

"Well I thought we could do all the touristy stuff today. Maybe see Notre Dame, The Louvre, Sacre-Coeur. I would have liked to go to Versailles, but I think it's a bit far out."

"Well let's go for breakfast downstairs and we could plot out a map of where to go. I know you love a good plan." I smile down at her.

She does love her order. I think one day has been enough for her to play it by ear. I knew I couldn't get away with it a second day of unplanned adventures. Yesterday she took it all in her stride, we just walked and talked, hand in hand and it gave me an idea of what being together would actually feel like. I think it did for her too, and I think that's why she pulled back a bit. But I get her point about it being difficult.

"I think we have something else to do before we get up though!" I hook my hand under her leg and pull her on top on me.

"We really don't have any time for these kinds of shenanigans," she says, and I frown as she moves off me and gets out of bed. "I need a shower." She walks off into the bathroom and I feel a pang of disappointment. Then she pokes her head around the door. "Are you coming in then?" I leap out of bed as fast as I can to join her.

When I go in, she's stood at the sink brushing her teeth, without trying to cover up or hide her body. She just seems so relaxed with herself. "Paris looks good on you!" I say from the door.

"Thanks!" She laughs, and I walk up behind her, pressing my front, not to mention my raging erection, to her back. I put one hand around her waist and with the other I move her hair off her shoulder, so I can kiss up her neck, before pulling her even closer.

"You smell amazing!"

"No, I smell of sex."

"That's what I said, you smell amazing!"

She pushes away from me and turns on the shower before stepping into the steamy spray. I quickly brush my teeth and follow her in, pressing myself up against her again. I pull her shower gel off the shelf and lather up my hands. Washing her is just a good excuse to put my hands all over her. I start at her shoulders and work my way down her front in circular movements, making the illusion of me washing her.

Her body is curvy in all the right places and as I wash over her, I squeeze her full breasts. She has complained about her post childbearing body, and if this is what she complains about, her body must have been something extra special beforehand. She calls her bum wobbly, but I call it juicy. It fills out a pair of jeans beautifully and right now I'm loving it as I'm grinding up against her.

I reach down, my soapy hands slide all the way up the inside of her thigh until I reach her centre and she lets out a soft moan, tilting her head back against my shoulder. I switch her leg and do the same again. I turn her to face me, wrapping my hands round her body to wash her back.

She returns the favour and starts with lathering up soap, then places her hands on my chest as she stares up at me. Once she's satisfied that part is clean, her hands dip down to wash the rest of my body and gradually make their way to my hardness, never breaking eye contact. Once she has finished, she moves her hands to wash my shoulders and hook them around my neck as I dip my head to kiss her.

As the kiss gets deeper, my need gets greater. I place my hands on her bum and pull her up as she wraps her legs around me. As I near her entrance, I pull back from the kiss. "Condom!" I say. She looks at me with an unrecognisable emotion.

"Well I haven't been with anyone else, and I can't get pregnant, so if you're clean then I'm ok with not using them." I look at her for a second, trying to compute what she just said.

"You know that I haven't been with anyone recently, and I have a health check every few months. The last one was just after we met." We stare at each other for a few moments and she nods, giving me the go ahead to push forward. Once I'm inside, we both still again and her head drops back as she lets out another little moan.

"This needs to be quick," she says, regaining her composure.

"Trust me beautiful, the way you feel right now, it's not going to be anything but quick," I growl out and start to move inside her. And all other thoughts just vanish from my head. She is all consuming.

Chapter Nineteen

We are sitting outside a small café, with two glasses of red wine, soaking up the Parisian atmosphere and taking the weight off our achy legs. It was a touristy kind of day today as Emma wanted to go and see places and things. And quite frankly I would have given her anything she wanted.

We had a guided tour around Le Louvre. We couldn't go it alone because neither of us has much clue about art. We both made the obligatory comment: "It's a lot smaller than I expected," about the Mona Lisa. We stood in front of the massive paintings by whichever artists it was. I actually wasn't listening because I was too busy watching Emma take it all in. Then we decided the best way to navigate Paris and see the most, was by boat up the Seine. It was my favourite part by far. It meant I could be with her, touch her, and not have to pretend I was interested in anything but her.

We've finished the touristy stuff for today and are just chilling, being together. She looks so relaxed and her beauty shines through. She's wearing her jeans and battered pumps, her sloppy jumper that's falling off her shoulders. Her hair is up in some kind of messy bun thing that leaves strands of hair all over the place. She is perfect imperfection and I never want this to end. We fly back tomorrow lunch time, and I know tonight is the last time I will see the unfiltered, easy, relaxed Emma for a while. Her brain will hit that organised-mum-on-a-mission stage, as the outside world starts to filter back in. So tonight, I am going to make the most of it.

She looks up at me as if my face has betrayed what I am thinking.

"What do you want to do this evening?" she asks. Just sit here and watch you for hours on end acting like a proper obsessed stalker?

"I'm not bothered. Anything you want," I say instead.

"There must be something. I've dictated where we've been today and it's our last evening here. We must do SOME-THING. We can't just do nothing."

"I would rather do nothing with you, than something with anyone else." But she narrows her eyes at me like I've just delivered the cheesiest line in the world. But in all fairness to me, it's 100% the truth. And then, as if some divine entity wanted to make me look like a liar, my phone vibrates in my pocket. I pull it out to see who is calling in case it is something I need to deal with, and then kill the call and put it back in my pocket.

"Who was that?" she asks. This could go either way. If I tell her it was nobody that will raise suspicions. If I tell her it was Ami that could also be bad. But she also may have seen the caller ID, so if I lie that could really blow up.

"It was just Ami," I say, trying to keep my tone light. But women can be funny about other women calling, and if I go into explaining our relationship that could also be taken the wrong way. There is absolutely nothing but friendship with us, but I just don't want to do anything that will upset what we have, or put doubt in Emma's mind about the way I feel about her.

"What did she want?" She is obviously trying not to sound annoyed or overthink things, but I can see in her eyes that her brain is running overtime.

"I don't know, I didn't answer it..." Now is not the time to get sarcastic. "...but it was probably confirming our dinner date." Shit! Date was definitely the wrong word to use there. "We meet up as friends every few weeks and go out for dinner for a catch up."

"Then why didn't you answer it?"

"Well that would have been rude, because I'm here with you."

"So you didn't want to arrange another DATE, while you were on this DATE," she says with a frown.

"It's not a date with Ami, we are just friends. We help each other out for functions and things." My words are coming out unusually fast and I think I'm starting to sweat.

"So its friends with benefits then."

"NO!" I practically shout and then I notice it. The corner of her mouth is hitched up, her tell that she's absolutely taking the piss out of me. "You're winding me up!" I say, and all the tension leaves my body. She just chuckles at me.

"You really went out of your way to explain that," she says, looking at me with wide eye., "I thought you might actually pass out. I bet she's really pretty!"

"Are you winding me up again? And no, she's average at best." I'm not going to tell her the truth that she's usually the best-looking woman in any room because that's a recipe for disaster. "Anyway, back to plans." I'm really trying to completely change the subject now but I've made it obvious and she just laughs.

"I'm not really bothered about going to a restaurant. We've been eating all day, there was a street vendor we passed earlier and it smelt amazing. Why don't we finish our drinks and head that way?"

Chapter Twenty

Well it has been an absolutely tortuous week. I said my goodbyes to Emma at the airport because she thought it would be best that I dropped her off quickly at home as she wasn't sure if the boys would be back yet. And since then I have pined for her. I've insisted on video calls instead of text because I don't want her to forget what I look like. I know that sounds ridiculous, but she has loads of other *stuff* going on. I just don't want her to forget. The phrase, *too much of a good thing*, is really ringing true.

I was spoilt with the amount of time I was able to spend with her in Paris and now I'm having withdrawal symptoms. The other mind fuck is that I knew that amount of time was a one off. And now there is no time in the immediate future that she can spare.

She's going out on a girls' night over the weekend and all kinds of things are running through my head. Will she meet anyone on this night out, like she met me in Edinburgh? Someone who could give her more? Someone who is nearer in age and geography? Why wouldn't she rather be spending time with me? So I'm hatching a really selfish plan to see her, but also let her have her girls' night out. I'm going to rope Sean in. We are going to drive down and infiltrate their night out, watch them get up to mischief, and at the end of the night I can at least see her in person.

"This has got all the potential to go dramatically wrong," Sean says when I explain my plan. And I know he's right. "You've even told me that you won't get a shag out of it because her boys aren't with their dad. So, what's the point?"

"The point, my dear friend, is that I am desperate to see her. Plus we have both experienced one of their *girls' nights* first hand, and that is something that is inducing real fear in me."

"You really like her then?"

"I think it's gone way further than like!"

"You think you are in love with her?" His face is overly shocked.

"Why is that so hard to believe?"

"Because a few months ago, you didn't date and you absolutely NEVER caught feelings."

"Well, things change."

"She must have one hell of a pussy!"

"Fuck off Sean!" The anger rising from me is palpable.

"Chill mate, I was just testing. I haven't seen you this screwed up about a woman since Victoria what's-her-face, in our first year." He gives me that knowing look. "You didn't eat for two weeks when you found out she'd snogged some other bloke."

"Yes, well, I thought Victoria Netball Captain was my soul-mate. I was heartbroken."

"Okay, so what's the plan? If we just gatecrash their night, they'll be pissed off. Even if Emma is happy to see you, you know the mates will be gunning for you."

"Yes I know. I definitely don't want to get on the bad side of Lizzie." I shudder just thinking of what she'd do to me. "So, I'm thinking we drive down there, stay out of the way, but watch them from afar."

"Like a proper stalker!" I ignore his comment.

"Then at the end of the night we say Hi. Then it's the best of both worlds. I've snooped on them, warned off any blokes sniffing around, they've had their girls' night and I get to be with Emma at the end of the night. And I'll get the unfiltered, drunk, carefree version."

"And what do I get out of all of this?"

"You don't get anything. You're my best mate. It's your job to go along with my crazy ideas. That's why you are currently raking it in at work!"

"Fair play!"

"No telling anyone. Especially Piers. He's got a big gob and he's in with the girls."

"Right! Find out where they are going and we'll go there incognito." Excellent, what could possibly go wrong?

Chapter Twenty-One

Emma

Tonight is the long-awaited girls' night. It's not as big a night out as Edinburgh was, especially as Sammy can't make it down. We've been waiting for a chance for us all to get together properly for a while. We are heading to our usual hang out – a relatively busy bar in town. It usually has a good mix of people and if we go early enough, we'll get some seats. I've decided to keep up making an effort because it makes me feel a bit more confident. So I have binned the jeans and a nice top tonight and gone for a floaty black dress, killer heels and my hair down in curls. I've done my make-up and I'm feeling good about my appearance. I take a quick selfie and send it to Ben.

He replies quickly with "Don't go chatting up any strange men!"

David doesn't have the boys this weekend, but he also hasn't made any kind of effort to sort out when he will have them either. So they are on their best behaviour and are staying at home. I'm going to try and be a calm mum and not check in on them every half hour.

I head out the door, shouting up to the boys who don't answer back, so I message them both to say I have left and absolutely no setting fire to the kitchen. Beth is waiting for me at the end of my drive as I lock the front door. She has volunteered her husband to be taxi tonight, as his mother is staying for the weekend and can watch the kids.

We'd already arranged the night out when Beth's mother-in-law said she was visiting, which Beth is very happy about because they don't really get on. It would have been nice for Beth and Steve to have a night out themselves, but his mother wants to spend time with her precious first born. I rolled my eyes when I heard that.

Lizzie is already in the back seat, so we just need to collect Megan. I hope there is no drama picking her up, because there often is. Her boyfriend is very over-protective. Well, that's how Megan describes him. A controlling arsehole is how Lizzie describes him. We pull up outside the house.

"Let me do the honours," Lizzie says as she gets out of the car and heads to the door.

We all know that there is only one person that Darren won't talk back to and that's Lizzie. She gets great pleasure from watching him squirm when he opens the door and she sends

Megan up the path first, so Darren can't get any sly digs in. He's done it before and she'll end up feeling awful about herself and she'll have a bad night.

We've arrived in enough time to the bar that it's not completely empty, but we can also bag the last set of seats. There's a low mahogany coffee table, surrounded by a leather sofa and two leather armchairs. Beth and Megan take the sofa and Lizzie heads to the bar. She reappears later with four glasses filled with ice and sets them down on the table.

"Erm have you forgotten something?" Beth says, looking at the glasses.

"You that desperate for a drink?" Lizzie replies, then points to the bar. "The over friendly barman took one look at you reprobates and said he'd carry them over." She settles herself into her seat and a fit young guy walks over to our table with four bottles of fruity cider.

"Here we go ladies," he says and Lizzie raises her eyebrows.

"Eeh thanks... Ollie," Beth says, looking at his name badge.

"I didn't realise you did table service in here..." Lizzie says, looking at poor Ollie. "Not very on brand for the Dog and Swan!"

"No we don't, but I thought I'd offer to help you lovely ladies." Beth is grinning from ear to ear at him, whereas Lizzie makes a vomiting motion and I have to stifle a laugh. "Enjoy!" Ollie walks back to the bar all full of himself.

"I've not seen him before," Beth says, practically drooling.

"You are virtually old enough to be his mother!" Lizzie has a point.

"I am not!"

"Quick maths Beth," I say bluntly. "He's probably only just legal, making you an 18-year-old mother. You probably went to school with his Mum," I say, laughing.

"Just because you are seeing a younger model."

"Yes, but he's not that young. We couldn't be mistaken for mother and son out on a date." Lizzie nearly spits out her drink at the thought.

"Megs, you've been quiet. You ok?" She looks up from her phone. No doubt she is getting messages about not drinking too much, not speaking to other men and not staying out too late, from Darren.

"Yeah, I'm ok." She puts her phone in her bag, knowing if she spends any more time looking at it, Lizzie will confiscate it like a miserable school teacher.

We chat about the ridiculous things our kids or partners have been up to and how the work week has gone. Then it's time for my round. I get up and head to the bar. Our usual bartender is there ready to serve me. He turns and looks at me for a minute before speaking.

"Well you look different!" He smiles and leans on the bar.

"Good different or bad different?" I have known Mitch for years, he's about the same age as me and has run the pub since I can remember.

"Good different! Of course." He takes another look at me and smiles. "You look..." He pauses trying to find his words. "Stunning... and happy."

"Are you trying to chat me up Mitch?" I'm joking with him and he knows it.

"Of course, same as always. Now what are you ladies drinking tonight? Fruity cider?"

"You know us!"

"Limey for Lizzie? Suits her personality! Berries for you? Although you are sweet enough." I give him an eye roll. "Megan and Beth have anything because after two they can't tell the difference."

"Jeez Mitch! Do we come in that often?" He laughs and gets the bottles out of the fridge. As his back is turned I feel a current in the air, as if someone is watching me. I look around. The bar has got a lot busier and there are people everywhere, but I can't quite pinpoint it. I pay for the drinks and take them back to our table.

I don't want to announce my feelings to the whole group because I think that will kick off Megan's paranoia. Not that her paranoia unfounded. Darren has been known to follow her to a bar or have his mates take pictures of her chatting to other men. Other men usually means something innocent, like a glass collector or someone asking to get past us. But it all fuels Darren's torment towards Megan. There's no telling her though. She's in love and we are just going to have to be here for the fall out that will inevitably come.

I lean into Lizzie while the other two are distracted. "Don't look round but I have a funny feeling we are being watched." Lizzie immediately looks round and I roll my eyes. "Why is it that whenever I say don't do something, that's the first thing you do. You're like a five-year-old." I laugh at her.

"Well I can't comment on something I haven't seen!" she says, and takes another look around. "Actually, I could have sworn I saw a familiar face at the bar."

"Who? Not Darren?"

"Nope!" She emphasises the 'p' on the end.

"Then who?"

"Well I thought I saw someone that looked like Sean, Ben's mate, but it seems unlikely."

"Hmm," I get my phone out and send a text to Ben asking what he's up to, but there's not the immediate reply, which is unusual. "Fancy a trip to the ladies, and on the way, you can do that thing you do."

"What thing?"

"You know, where you take in everything without anyone knowing."

"I'll bring out my inner detective," she says to me and turns to the others. "We're just heading to the toilet." We both stand and manoeuvre our way through the crowd of people until we get through the doors to the toilets. Once the door is closed, we can start the debrief.

"Well?"

"Oh yes, they are here alright. Ben and Sean, wearing baseball caps to disguise themselves. They are standing at the far end of the bar. Ben has his back towards our table. There's not much of a line of sight between the two but it's enough to keep a watch. Enough to spy on anyone who goes to the bar."

"And there she is, the inner detective!"

"What now then? How do you want to play this?"

"Well I don't know. On one hand I'd love to see him and its nice he's made the effort."

"And on the other?"

"On the other is a *what the fuck* moment."

"So we're gonna mess with them, right? PLEASE say we're gonna mess with them."

"Hell yes. But I'll need to think about how."

We make our way out of the toilets and head back through the bar nearly bumping into a tall dark figure.

"Hey. Emma?" The man is looking straight down at me.

"Hey Alex. It's been forever!"

"You look amazing as ever."

"Why thanks, so do you. You look so much taller."

"Maybe you are smaller. We should get a drink and catch up sometime," he says with a little laugh.

"Yes, that would be lovely. Actually Alex, I know that this is a bit rude of me, but can I ask a favour?"

"Well that really depends." He raises an eyebrow and I set out explaining.

We head back to our table and carry on our conversations with the girls for a few minutes, then I get up and head to the bar. Alex is waiting to be served and I stand next to him with my back towards Ben. In a loud, over exaggerated way, Alex starts to chat to me. He's obviously done this before, as there is arm touching and everything. Lizzie said she'd keep an eye on the boys to gauge their reactions and intervene if she thought it might get messy. I look over to her and she gives me a wide eye and sits up ramrod straight. That means they have seen and are paying attention.

Alex offers to buy me a drink and there is movement to the side of me. All of a sudden, Ben is there pressing up against my back, his firm body like a brick wall.

"What the fuck is going on here?" His tone is clipped. I can tell his anger is simmering below the surface, and within seconds Lizzie is also there. But I don't need to say anything because to the side of Alex steps another man who wraps his arm around him and kisses him on the lips.

"This," I say pointing next to me, "is Alex, an old friend of mine. And this…" I point to the other man, "is Alex's boyfriend. Sorry we haven't been introduced. I'm Emma and this…" gesturing my thumb over my shoulder, "is my… idiot, Ben!" I point to Sean who has joined the group. "And this is his equally stupid sidekick, Sean."

"I'm Danny." He puts his hand out and I take it to shake. "Nice to meet you, Emma." I turn round to face Ben.

"For two intelligent, driven and also super sexy guys, you are very bloody stupid." Both of them look down like children being scolded.

"Can I just explain?" Ben looks at me with his puppy eyes.

"No, I'm not sure you can!"

"Please." He grabs hold of my elbow to pull me towards the door. I take it he doesn't want to grovel in front of an audience.

We make our way outside and as the cool air hits my face, he turns me towards him. "I'm really sorry. I don't know what I was thinking." I give him a stern look and fold my arms over my chest. I'm definitely not taking that as an answer. After he gathers his thoughts, he starts again. "Okay, I did know what I was thinking but that doesn't mean it was a coherent thought.

I remember the last girls' night you had. Plus I wanted to see you really badly. But on the other hand I didn't want to crash your girls' night because I know it is important to you." I'm still looking at him sternly. "Again I'm really sorry."

"This night out is nothing like Edinburgh, for a start. And you didn't need to spy on us. You could have said hi, gone for a drink and come back later and that would have been fine. But no!" He looks so fed up, I think he realises his mistake. But I have to reiterate why it's not acceptable behaviour. "Listen, what you did in there smacks of control. I don't think you understand what Megan is going through right now. Her boyfriend does exactly what you did just then. But then he punishes her for it."

"I'm sorry. I didn't know." And right on cue, Megan rushes out of the pub followed by Sean.

"What's happened?" I ask, knowing full well it has something to do with Darren. Her eyes are full of unshed tears and her hand shakes as she shows me what's on screen. It's a picture of her looking up to the barman who brought over our drinks. The picture makes it look like she's flirting with him, which is not what happened at all.

The words underneath the picture say *what the fuck is going on here!!!!!*

"Oh Megs!" I envelop her in my arms. After a few moments I pull her back and hold her at arm's length. "We all know that is not how it looks, and so does he I bet. PLEASE let us help you get away from that man."

"I can't. He's not always like this."

"No? Just every time you go out or do something that's not with him."

"I'm sorry for ruining the night."

"You haven't ruined anything, don't you dare." I know that if she blames herself then it will be another thing that he can hold over her when we want to go out again.

"I need to get home." Her eyes cast down to the floor. "I'll get a taxi."

"I'll take you." Sean buts in without hesitation. "I'm the designated driver."

"Thanks, but if you drop me off it will make everything a million times worse."

"I can drop you in the next street, so he doesn't know. But if I don't take you, I'll be worried about you all night."

"Yes, go on. I'll be happier with Sean taking you. Just tell Darren you are getting a cab."

"He'll check my phone..." she doesn't finish the sentence sensing she has said too much. I take out my phone and type a message. Her phone beeps and she reads it and smiles. It says:

Emma: Just popped to the toilet. I've ordered you a taxi, it'll be outside in 5 minutes.

"Ready?" She nods to Sean as he takes her elbow and steers her to the carpark at the back of the pub. I drop her another message.

Emma: Message when you get home

"I had no idea."

"Why would you? It's not something we all shout about. We've tried to get her to leave him, but she won't. But I think it is starting to get dangerous and I'm worried about her. I know everyone thinks I get treated badly by David, but this is next level."

"Is there anything I can do?"

"Not at the minute. We're just waiting for the fall out. I may need some property help in the not-so-distant future."

"Anytime. And I am really sorry. Do you forgive me?" He wraps he arms around me and looks down at me with those puppy eyes again.

"Yes, I suppose..." Before I have even finished, he has dipped his head and landed a kiss. He moves one hand and threads it along my jaw, tilting my head so he can get deeper and better access. The butterflies start in my stomach and all the annoyance is washed away. I pull away, trying to get some air.

"You know that bar chat was a set up. Lizzie had already clocked you."

"Serves me right, I suppose."

"Can we go back in and have a drink together, rather than you lurking in the shadows?" He laughs, and we make our way back inside.

I head to the bar and he heads to the bathroom. The bar is busy tonight but I manage to get Mitch's attention and order our drinks. I feel someone very close beside me and I know it's not Ben. I turn to face what turns out to be a drunken, leary man.

"Well hello sweetheart." I just roll my eyes at him. "Fancy coming home with me for a good time?"

He then proceeds to put his hand up the back of my skirt. As I push him off there's a rush of bodies. Out of nowhere Ben has hold of this guy by the neck of his t-shirt, gathered up in his fist and his arm drawn back, whilst simultaneously pushing me out of the way. The blow lands and there's a splattering of blood. In an instant Mitch has rounded the bar and is trying to pull them a part. Sean appears from behind, returning from dropping off Megan, and pulls Ben back.

Mitch looks between the two of them to work out what has happened. I grab him by the arm to explain the situation. Without hesitation he pulls at the bloke and drags him towards the door. Pointing at Ben, he yells, "calm the fuck down!" and carries on out of the door.

The tension in the air is palpable. The rage on Ben's face, matched with the heaving of his chest, shows the fire is still there. I just want to neutralise the situation and calm him down before Mitch reappears and throws us out too. I lay my hand on his chest and the built-up fury dissipates.

"I'm okay. Just calm yourself down," I say softly.

"For fuck's sake, I leave you for five minutes and you get yourself in a fight." I'm not sure this intervention from Sean is going to help.

Mitch powers back into the room on a mission. He bypasses Ben and faces me, putting his hands on my shoulders.

"You okay?" I nod and he turns his attention to Ben. "I get why you punched him, but I don't like violence in my pub. Either calm down or leave."

"He's calm," I say to Mitch. I hand Ben his drink and direct him to the table, where Lizzie and Beth are still sitting.

We sit in an awkward silence until Lizzie breaks the tension. "Well that escalated quickly. You know she could have handled it herself right!"

Sean looks between the girls. "Does this happen often."

"More often than you'd think." Beth starts. "The stories we could tell you. I bet if you asked the women in here whether something similar had ever happened to them, every one of them would give you a story." The conversation carries on between them and Ben turns to look at me. We are sitting close on the sofa, Sean perched on the arm beside Ben.

"I'm sorry," he says quietly, cupping my face in his hand.

"I know."

"You shouldn't have to. I wasn't trying to be all possessive or anything."

"But I can fight my own battles. You just need to be my support, not my saviour." He kisses me on the lips and we both relax and turn back to the conversation. This night has turned out completely differently from how I imagined it would.

Chapter Twenty-Two

It's 5.30pm and I have just walked through the door of my house. It doesn't look the same as when I left because it looks like someone has broken in. I know from the things all over the floor that, in fact, it is just that the boys are home.

There are shoes, a coat, two bags, one of which is open and has its content trailing up the stairs. A blazer and a tie hang precariously from the banister, half a school sandwich sticking out of one pocket. It's anyone's guess how long it's been there.

I walk through the hall into the kitchen living space, and the counter top is covered. There's spilt milk and what I can only assume is milkshake powder. The bread packet is open with slices hanging out, the butter is open with a knife daggered out the top. The fridge has been closed over but is beeping because it's not actually closed and is letting out all the cold air. Clean washing lays strewn all over the floor, pulled from the dryer by someone in search of something.

"For Fuck's sake," I mutter. I start tidying it up as I usually do. This is a daily occurrence so it's not a surprise. Then I stop, mid clothes gathering, and think what the hell am I doing? I go back to the hall and shout the boys from the bottom of the stairs. There is no answer! I call them individually but get no answer. Right, I think, I've had enough of this shit!

I walk back to the living room and flick off the power to the internet router. I wait a few minutes and hear the pitter patter of not so tiny feet upstairs and a rush of bodies down the stairs.

"MMMuuummmmm..." they say, not quite in unison.

"The Wi-Fi has gone off!" Joshua is obviously the most perturbed by this.

"I know the Wi-Fi is off, I bloody turned it off! Didn't you hear me calling you?" I stand facing them with arms folded, mummy face on. "What the actual fuck is all this mess!" I start my rant. The two, nearly men, stare at me like rabbits caught in headlights. They never see me lose my shit, and I never swear directly at them. "Sort it out right this second! Kitchen too!" They are dumb struck by my outburst, but I'm not backing down. "Go on then!" I shout and they move into action, picking up their stuff and rushing about.

After about ten minutes of mayhem, I've turned the router back on and they've picked up everything and put things away. They rush up to their rooms and I stand at the bottom of the stairs waiting for the outcry.

"Mum what's the Wi-Fi password? It's changed." Noah this time, asking from the landing.

"Tidy your room," I reply.

"Oh Mum…" he bites back. I just point him to his bedroom and he slopes off. Joshua goes through the same motions but I can hear him mumbling profanities under his breath as his slams his door behind him.

Twenty minutes pass and both of them saunter into the living room and stand over me while I sit, watching the news.

"Mum! Can we have the password now?"

"Tidy your room," I say again.

"We have tidied our rooms…" an exasperated Noah says.

"Capital T, no spaces." I'm trying to keep from smirking. They are still standing over me, obviously trying to compute what I just said. I look at them. "The Wi-Fi password is Tidyyourroom." Realisation finally dawns on their faces and they sulk back up to their rooms with "Not funny, mum!" mutterings.

Emma 1 Delinquent teenagers 0!

I'm proper pleased with myself, when my phone pings. I look down to see a message from Sammy that just says "SOS". I frown. It's never usually Sammy who has emergencies. I pick my phone up and dial her straight away.

"Em!" She answers with a sob.

"Sammy, what's happened?" Her tears are uncontrollable and I have a mild panic. "Take a deep breath…" I wait to hear her exhale. "Now another one!" I wait again. "Now tell me who I need to kill!"

"Ah Emma! I've been so stupid." The sobs start again.

"Okay! Well, we can fix stupid… generally."

"I'm pregnant!" She starts sobbing again. I don't need to sugar coat it.

"Ah shit!" With any of my other friends, I would gauge how happy they were with the situation, but there's no need with her. She has never shown any indication of maternal desire. She looks at babies with distain and was always *Fun Aunt Sammy*.

"I can't keep it. You know how I feel about kids."

"My kids put you off for life?" I laugh.

"No! ...Well yes, yours and everyone else's."

"Do you know who the father is?"

"I think so! But it's complicated." It always is. "I used protection, I'm on the pill, but I was sick a few months ago, had to have a course of antibiotics. Do you remember?"

"Oh yeah. So what's the plan." I know exactly what the plan is, I just need to know the timings.

"I've booked an appointment at a clinic."

"Do you want me to come with you?" She starts sobbing again and I wait for the answer.

"Would you?"

"Of course! You are my best friend. I would do anything for you. I just need to get things here sorted. When is it?"

"Day after tomorrow. Please don't tell anyone else!"

"Of course not! Leave it with me to sort out and I'll let you know when I'm coming."

"Thanks Em."

"Are you gonna be ok? Do you need to talk more?"

"No! I'm gonna get in the bath with a bottle of wine."

"Okay, but just one though!" We say bye and I hang up the phone. I'll make something to eat and think of what I'm going to do. It's the middle of the week so I'm probably going to have to bite the bullet and ask David.

It has been a long day. I'm just starting to relax after being on the phone to what seems like everyone. I have booked emergency holidays for Thursday and Friday with work. I have managed to convince David to come and stay at mine from tomorrow evening, so I can drive up to Edinburgh after work. It took a lot of convincing but having them go to his on a school night would be all kinds madness – moving of clothes, bags etc – and they can easily get the bus from home but not from David's. I fire off a quick message to Ben because I'm just too mentally exhausted to speak anymore.

Me: Hiya! I'm too tired to talk but I needed to let you know something.

Ben: Hey Babe, what's up?

Me: I'm coming up to Edinburgh tomorrow. But I can't meet up...

The dots start for a reply, then stop and then start again. I feel like it's going to be a long message.

Ben: Okay!

Me: There's something I need to do with Sammy. Please don't ask me what!

Ben: Right!

What kind of answer is 'right'?

Ben: Do you need me to pick you up from the station? Or drive down to get you?

Me: No I'm gonna drive up myself after work.

The dots start again, then stop. He's obviously answering then changing his mind.

Ben: Fine

It seems very much far from fine, I think, but I can't be bothered with another argument. So I leave it.

He's obviously been mulling everything over for the past few hours and as I get into bed and go to put my phone on silent, a message pings up from him.

Ben: Will you let me know when you have set off to-morrow and when you get here? I understand you can't see me but I'd like to know you are safe.

Me: Of course x

I have to let Ben think about things before wanting an answer. I get the impression his first response is explosive, but once he has thought about it, he can see another side and is much more reasonable. I like that he thinks about how his response may affect me. Not many others do. I feel safe to tell him how I feel and what's happening without him kicking off. I know he will have wanted to see me. I know that his first response would have been questioning why I'd go all the way up there and not see him, when he came all the way to see me. And I'm a little disappointed that the first chance I get to go to Scotland, it won't be to visit him. But Sammy takes priority.

I rush home from work. I packed my bag last night, but I wanted to come back to the house before David gets here. I want to make sure he turns up, but also to check round the house to make sure there aren't things *out of place* that he can pick at. He doesn't even live here anymore, so he has no right. But I just don't have the headspace for him now.

I've made sure there is enough food in the house because David is incapable of thinking or doing for other people, especially the boys. I can't think of anything else left to do, but I'm wondering whether to hide my underwear because David has started to say some creepy things of late. I push the thought out of my head and go and say my goodbyes to the boys. As I head back downstairs, I can see David's car pull up. Before he can even reach the door I'm out and unlocking the car. I don't want to engage in any kind of conversation with him that will wind me up before my long drive.

Before I can avoid him, David is up in my face. "What mess is Sammy in now then?" He's never liked Sammy much, even at university. Maybe because she thought he was a dick. To be fair, she was right. But when you're young and in love, you don't see any of their flaws.

"She's not in any mess, she just needs some support."

"And that always has to come from you?" He spits the words. "When you've got responsibilities here?"

"She's my best friend. And I'm quite sure the boys will survive in your capable hands." I get in the car before he can think of a comeback and reverse out of the drive. He just stands there with his hands on his hips. I drive around the corner and pull up to send Ben a quick message to say I've set off and get a message straight back saying *stay safe* and a heart emoji. And it's such a different sentiment from the one I've just left, I blow out a breath before I start the car again.

Chapter Twenty-Three

Joshua

Well this is going to be fun. NOT!

Mum rushed off to see Sammy after work. She came home, mainly just to pick up her things and make sure my dad had shown up. He has a habit of letting everyone down at the last minute, but he'll go on like a dick if anyone lets him down.

Whatever is going on with Sammy it must be serious because mum never leaves us through the week. Dad is too busy to have us, so we go to his every other weekend. Actually, we don't. We probably go once a month on average because *something has come up* quite often. Mum doesn't remind us which weekends we go now. There's no point because it's generally rearranged.

She won't say what's wrong with Sammy, but there have been hushed phone calls and quick hang ups.

I did wonder if it was her new boyfriend that she was going to see. He's Scottish. But I doubt she'd leave us to see him. He's actually an alright guy. He came to the house looking for mum one evening a bit ago. She wasn't in. She was taking Noah somewhere, but I answered the door – I wouldn't normally but mum said there was a delivery due.

He has the new Lamborghini Huracan. It is awesome. V10 engine, dual clutch transmission, it's dope. He let me have a sit in it and start the engine. I would have loved to have driven it, but he had to go. And from the phone call I heard, my mum went mad with him. I think he's meant to be a secret and she hadn't known he was coming. He was *in the area*, which I very much doubt. He was also surprised I answered the door, but I knew kind of who he was.

She tries to keep things from us but she's so obvious. She has stupid puppy eyes when he sends her a message. But, she has been generally happier, in a lot better mood. A bit stricter too, which is a pain in the ass, but we've had it easy. She tricked us into tidying our rooms the other day. I was fuming, but well played, I suppose.

Then there was that weekend that dad just didn't turn up and she lost her shit. She paced about ranting to her friends. She usually just takes his shit, but not this time. We got shipped out the next day to Lizzie's for a sleepover, as if we were six years old. I complained a lot, but to be fair I had nearly burnt the house down the night before. The upside was seeing Sienna, my oldest friend, apparently. We may as well have been born in the same hospital room. She's like a sister to me – annoying and I mainly hate her. We don't see that much of each other now, but when we do, usually when there's a celebration, she gives me a girl's perspective on all the shit that goes on. And all my mates fancy her, so I've got bragging rights. I quite enjoyed telling them I'd spent the night with Sienna. They were raging.

Dad has been here about two hours, we've had takeaway pizza for tea and he has been as annoying as usual. Any little thing he kicks off about, just cos he's ancient and has forgotten what it's like being my age. You know the kind of stuff he says, *why do you have to be online all the time, when I was a lad...blah blah* and my all-time favourite is *that music is just random noises and shouting!*

He's also started the interrogation about what mum has been up to. Generally, she doesn't get up to much, but I won't tell him about her boyfriend because he'll go on something ridiculous. I don't know why he's so bothered about what she's doing. He treated her like shit before he dumped her and has a long line of giggly woman that he parades around. So why does he still need to be ass? I don't even know why we still go over there. I mean, Noah still kind of hero worships him, and Dad acts like he couldn't give a shit about us. I don't think he knows anything about who we are or what we do. He goes on about school and good exam results and *pulling my finger out*, whatever that means.

"Josh!" Great. Here we go again! I find him going through the drawers in the kitchen and then onto the living room looking through the book shelf.

"Looking for something?" I ask.

He doesn't answer the question directly. "Has your mother been seeing anyone?" Here we go! His face is screwed up and he's getting redder and more impatient as he searches.

"What makes you ask that?" I'm not telling him what I know, he'll just torture Mum. He'll tell her she's not good enough and things that will make her doubt her own self-worth. He does it all the time at the smallest thing.

"Do you know anyone with the initial B?" He looks like a crazy man, pulling out books and flicking through the pages, as if trying to find something hidden.

Noah walks in and says, without hesitation, "Oh that'll be Ben!" He beams, knowing that he got to answer a question. Well Noah has obviously picked up on that well-kept secret. Mum is going to go mad.

"WHO is Ben?" Dad asks the question through gritted teeth.

"Just someone Mum speaks to," Noah replies. He shrugs and walks out.

Dad has gone a funny colour, like a reddish purple, looks like he's gonna have a heart attack. He looks back at me and hands me a little card. "Do you know anything about this?" I look down, it looks like those cards you get in flowers to say who they are from. It says *Thanks for this weekend, hope to do it again soon, B x*. I look up and shrug. He hands me another, that says *Looking forward to seeing you, B x* I shrug again. "Has your mother been seeing someone?" he says again.

What is it to him? It's really pissed me off now. I wouldn't say it to her face, but Mum does everything for us. She covers up when Dad is being a dick, she hasn't paraded every new boyfriend. Dad introduces all of his girlfriends as if we're getting a new step mum!

I just can't help myself. He's just pressing all my buttons now. "Yes actually, she has. He's a really cool bloke, nice job, nice house, drives a nice car, Lamborghini actually. He's a good laugh. And he sends her flowers all the time." Okay half of that I have maybe elaborated on just to wind him up, especially the flowers bit because I never remember Dad sending her any...

"How dare she..." He starts ranting but I just can't be arsed with the dramatics. I walk out of the room and go upstairs, noise cancelling headphones should do the trick. I don't think he's even noticed. I can still hear him ranting from up here.

Chapter

Twenty-Four

Emma

It's been a slow journey full of traffic with just one stop for a cup of coffee and a toilet break. I pull into Sammy's building complex and into her designated parking spot. My battered old car stands out like a sore thumb, but I don't really care. She's dependable and I don't have too much of that sometimes. I get my bag out of the car and head into the building for Sammy to buzz me in, dropping Ben a quick message.

I meet her at her door and she collapses into my hug, sobbing. I don't usually see Sammy like this. She is the strong one of us. She's in joggers and a holey jumper, no make-up and her hair in a messy, messy bun! Sammy is usually so put together, as if she just wakes up with perfect make-up and hair.

"Let's get you inside and you can tell me what's going on."
There's definitely more to this than just Sammy falling pregnant. I take Sammy and my bag inside, deposit Sammy on the sofa and head to the kitchen to make a cuppa. I hear her quietly sobbing as I bring in our tea and sit next to her.

"Come on then! Spill!" She looks at me again and starts crying.

"What a mess!" She takes in a few stuttered breaths before starting to explain. "You know I told you about that guy I started a thing with?" I nod. "Well he's married."

"Oh Sammy! And the baby is his?"

"Yes. But the added kicker is that he was having an affair because he and his wife weren't getting on."

"They all say that!"

"Yeah, but they weren't getting on because of the strain that fertility treatment was having on their relationship. She can't get pregnant and now he's got me pregnant."

"Shit! Have you told him about the baby?"

"How can I? There's absolutely no way I'm keeping it, and from what he's been saying, she's gone all baby crazy and would do anything to have one. Talked about a surrogate and everything. I don't want to become their incubator."

"Well that's... tricky!"

"To say the least. I've cut contact but he's going to want to know why I have fallen silent all of a sudden."

"Can you say you have been busy with work and had no time?" She gives me a very sheepish look. "Oh Sam, please tell me you don't work with him." She nods as the tears start all over again.

"But I also really like him."

"Well if you aren't going to tell him the truth, you are gonna need to tell him a lie. One that's convincing. That shouldn't be too hard, you are a lawyer. Don't you lie for a living?"

"Like what, my dog's dead...he knows I don't have a dog!"

"Your Nan died?"

"But his Nan has just died!"

"You have some kind of illness?"

"He'll want to come and look after me!"

"A contagious disease then?" She just looks at me with a frown. "Gonorrhoea?"

"Not funny!"

"Meningitis?... Tuberculosis? ... The Black Death?" She eventually laughs.

"You have to remember that he is also a lawyer and can see straight through any lie."

"So we are swinging back to the truth then."

"Not happening!"

"What about after the event? So there is no need to discuss possibilities?"

"I don't know if he would ever forgive me."

"What about a miscarriage?"

"I think I would feel worse for the false sympathy."

"Well you'll need to tell him something, or maybe just leave the country. Emigrate to Peru!"

Sammy's phone starts to ring on the table and she looks at the caller ID. "It's him!"

"Peru it is then! Answer the phone and just say I'm here and I'm in crisis."

"He'll hear that something is wrong."

"Then text. Fuck's sake Sammy, you need to do something, or he'll be round here!" She picks up her phone and types a message.

Sammy: Sorry can't talk, Emma's here having a crisis'
JP: Okay! U OK? You're not at work
Sammy: I'm fine... Emma's not, girl's stuff.
JP: Right, speak later?
Sammy: Yep

"At least that gives you some breathing space. You can say you can't talk about it because it's not your story to tell." She nods. "What do men think 'girl's stuff' actually means? They never question it."

"Probably periods and then they have some kind of notion that our whole insides fall out once a month."

"Idiots! Well at least it gives us an excuse. What time is your appointment?"

"9:30."

"Why don't we get some sleep and maybe go for breakfast after the appointment?"

"Sounds like a plan." She stands, picks her stuff up and heads to her bedroom. She stops and turns towards me. "Thanks Em. Love you!"

"Love you!" I pick up my bags and head to Sammy's spare room.

Her place is so posh I may as well be staying in a hotel. I take a shower, mainly because the jets on it are so amazing, but the heat will also help me sleep. I take out my phone to set an alarm for the morning and see Ben has messaged. I press the call button and he answers almost immediately.

"Hi Princess!"

"Hi."

"You ok? How was the drive?"

"I'm good, just a bit tired. It was rush hour and the traffic was terrible. I just wanted to hear your voice before I went to sleep."

"It's good to hear you too." I can tell by his voice he is smiling. "How's Sammy? Do you know how long you'll stay?"

"She's not great. I'm gonna see how things pan out. I can't stay too long, because how would a grown man and two teenagers manage for a few days without me?" I say sarcastically.

He laughs "I don't think I would manage without you either."

"You're managing now!"

"Doesn't mean I want to."

"Are you becoming needy, Mr Ambrose?"

"Yes, very! Anyway, I'll let you get some rest. Can we speak tomorrow?"

"Yes. I'll call in the evening maybe. Goodnight!" There's a long pause as if he wants to say something else, but eventually he signs off.

"Night Princess!"

I put my phone on silent, plug it into the charger and lay down. I'm so tired, I should just close my eyes and drift off but this is the time I start to overthink things.

I'm up early, I've got dressed and I wander into the kitchen where Sammy stands at the counter with a coffee in her hand.

"Coffee?"

"Always!" I reply as she pours out the dark liquid. I'm more of a tea drinker, but I just need a coffee-type caffeine shot to start the day, especially this morning.

"We'll get the tram to the clinic. It's just a few stops."

"Okay. How are you feeling about everything?"

"I don't know. Confused! Not about the pregnancy. I'm definitely not having this baby, or any baby for that matter." She blows out a sigh. "But what does it mean for me and JP? It was all just casual and now I think I may have caught feelings!"

"Oh no! You don't do feelings!" I smirk at her. She's always been the love them and leave them kind of girl. A quick hook up or a weekend away and she's had her fill. This is really the first time she's liked a bloke since our university years, and it has come with all kinds of complications.

"Come on, let's make tracks," she says, picking up her bag. I down my coffee and follow her out.

We get to the clinic and it isn't what I was expecting. Although I'm not sure what I was expecting. We may as well be going to the podiatrist. We go in and Sammy gives her name. She is given paperwork to fill out and we both take a seat in the waiting area.

We sit in a weird, subdued mood until Sammy is called in through the double door by someone who looks like a beautician.

"Do you want me to come in with you?"

"No, I'll be fine."

I nod as she disappears through the door. I take my phone out of my bag and check for any messages from the boys, then send a quick message to Ben.

Me: Hey, hope your day is going well.

Ben: It's better now!

Me: Can't really talk but I just wanted to say hi. It feels weird being so close yet not seeing you.

Ben: ☹ I know but you are there to be a friend.

I smile at his response. If this was David when we were first seeing each other he would be pulling out all the guilt right now. I know it pains him not to see me, I could hear it in his voice yesterday. He tried to mask it with a joke, but I could still tell.

Sammy comes out after about 20 minutes.

"What's the verdict?"

She sighs. "I am really early so, I need to take tablets to induce it. I took one in there and I have another to take in 24-48 hours' time. And that's it done."

"I think we deserve a slap-up breakfast now then." I smile up to her and she gives me a small smile that. She's not as tough as she says. We head out and find a café that does a full Scottish breakfast and we go for the works. I know I'll not finish even half of it, but I don't care. The food will give us more time to talk. Sammy talks me through what the nurse explained. She wants to have a bit of space tomorrow, so we talked about plans for the next two days.

"Let's not talk about this anymore," Sammy starts. "It's bloody depressing. I want to talk about you and that Mr fitty CEO."

"You make him sound like some like one of those grumpy bosses in those smutty books you read."

"Well, is he?"

"No not at all. He's a down to earth CEO running a company with his mates."

"But also earning millions?"

"Well, yes!"

"I want to know all about Paris."

"I'm pretty sure you don't want to know ALL about Paris!"

"I absolutely do! Every last smutty detail."

"Well I'm not really a kiss and tell kind of girl, but..."

"I knew it! He's a fucking sex machine isn't he?"

"Hell yeah," I giggle, and it's true. I really don't usually tell people about my sex life. I don't know whether it was because I was married, and that kind of stuff needed to be kept in the confines of our bedroom. Or whether it was because my friends knew David, or that the sex just wasn't much to talk about. It was probably a bit of all of them.

"Come on, you need to tell me now. You can't just dangle that bit of tea and not deliver."

"Where do I start? He's unbelievably sexy, whispers dirty things in my ear whilst in the full throws."

"You don't call him Daddy do you?"

"Oh god no!" I make a retching face. "He's ten years younger than me for a start. He's kind of dominant but not the *get on your knees and suck my cock* kind of dominant."

Sammy's face is shocked. "Emma Lowther, I have never heard such filth come from your mouth... I fucking love it!"

"But he has given me orgasms that I never knew I could have." Her eyes widen, and I laugh. She makes a hand movement encouraging me to explain further. "Well, I have never had a vaginal orgasm before. Well, before Ben, I mean."

"What?"

"In fact, I don't remember having many of any kind orgasm with David."

"Well that's just sad. I'm glad you are catching up now. And some women just can't orgasm that way, so he's definitely doing something right."

"I think because it's not forced, not expected." I lean in towards her over my plate of food and lower my voice. "He even made me come using his fingers, just sitting in his car on our first date."

"You dirty little minx." Sammy laughs, which makes me chuckle too.

"I just feel so comfortable around him. He's so sexy, but its more than that. I think it's that I feel seen. Do you know what I mean? I haven't really explained it well."

"I know what you mean! He's there for you and not him."

"That's exactly it. But it's more than the sex. I actually really like him. He makes me feel ..." I look around, searching for the right word. "I don't know... Treasured, I suppose."

"That's really nice, and exactly what you need. Someone who is there for you and not the one-sided relationship that you had, in fact still have, with David. You giving all the time and him just taking. Mainly taking the piss!"

I give her the look I always do when she talks that way about David. The *I know but he's the father of my kids so leave it* look.

But I also say, "You are absolutely right." Sammy looks shocked at my response. "And you know what? Things are going to have to change. I need to get my life back." Then I remember something that puts a smile on my face. "You know, a few days after I came back from Paris, I got a postcard from Ben." She gives me a quizzical look. "Yes, he must have ducked out, bought the card and posted it without me knowing."

"Awww, that's so lovely."

"It said, *Wish you were here, B x* because he knew that we are trying to keep things under wraps. Especially when he popped in unannounced the other week."

"He didn't! He couldn't have been *just passing*. He lives miles away."

"Yes! And I wasn't in but Joshua was!" She pulls a face. "Yes I know. And Josh got all *nice car* with him. Had a good old chin wag. I went mental on Ben."

"You don't want him to meet the boys?"

"I do, eventually! But I want to be able to manage it myself. Because if the boys know, then David will know and I haven't quite gauged his reaction yet."

"What does it matter what David thinks? He's the one who buggered off!"

"I know, but you know me. I just want a quiet life. And let's face it, David will turn the whole situation round and make it all about him."

She gives me the look that say she knows I'm right. I'm not quite ready for us to go public yet. I need to know how the boys feel about me being in another relationship. I need them to know that I will always put them first.

Chapter

Twenty-Five

I blow out a breath as I sit in my car contemplating the last few days. Sammy wants her own space for a bit and I don't blame her. She's taken her second lot of medication and I'll need to check on her in a few hours. I think she wants me to head home, but there's absolutely no way I'm leaving her. I will give her some space.

It's Saturday lunchtime, and although I have told Ben I couldn't see him while I was up, I feel like if I don't see him to at least say hello, I might break. He's been more understanding about me being here than I would if it was the other way around. We have had a few messages but that's it. I'm torn because I want to see him, but I don't want to leave Sammy too long. And tomorrow I'll have to get back to whatever nightmare is waiting for me back home.

I've not really heard from David as such, but Joshua has messaged me asking when I'm coming home when usually he doesn't care whether I'm there or not. I have an uneasy feeling about the whole situation if I'm honest. I just can't quite put my finger on it.

I'll call Ben, see what's going on with him and I'll make my decision then.

He answers in one ring, "Hey Princess! You ok?"

"Yes, I'm good. Just getting a bit of headspace. I thought I'd distract myself and see what you have got going on." I think it's a bit unfair to ask him to drop everything, just because I've changed my mind about seeing him.

"Well not much really. I'm in the office today."

"On a Saturday? Get you mister workaholic."

He gives a little chuckle. "That's me! I have some work I need to get done before start of play Monday, and I'm thinking about putting in a game of rugby tomorrow."

"I didn't know you played rugby!"

"Not as often as I'd like. It keeps me in shape."

"Tell me more!"

"It's just the local team. I sometimes sponsor them, and in return they let me tap in on a few games because they know I can't commit to being on a team full time."

"Ah now I've got all kinds of images running through my head. I had a bit of a thing for rugby players in my Uni days."

"Did you now?"

"Oh yeah, short shorts, muscles, mud and bruises. What's not to love!" I laugh. "The best thing was they were big softies really and used to fall for my little lady puppy eyes all the time. It was hilarious."

"That sounds like a story I need to hear."

"Maybe another time. Are you on your own in the office?"

"Sean said he might pop in later to run some reports." There's a pause and I know the question is coming. "So when are you heading home?"

"I'm not sure. Sammy says she's okay, but she's clearly not. I'm not going to take her word for it because she's putting on a brave face. But I'll definitely need to be heading home soon."

"I think you're doing the right thing. If you think she needs you, you're probably right. Just let me know when you set off back, so I know you are safe."

"Okay, I've got to go. Speak soon!" I hang up before he can answer so I don't give the game away.

That conversation, the fact that he didn't push to see me, that he just wanted me to do what I needed to and be safe, has sparked the need to see him and kiss him. I google his office address and put it in the sat nav.

Thirty minutes later, after lots of traffic, nearly going down a one-way street the wrong way and trying to find a parking space, I am at his office. I rang Sean to ask how I could get into the office without blowing the surprise. He spoke to security and gave me the codes for the internal doors.

The offices are in a large glass and steel building. Ambrose Holdings share space on the 7th floor. I've tried to be as quiet as possible coming in through their main office door. There's an empty reception desk and I head down the corridor to his office. The office is large and has mainly windows onto the corridor.

The blinds are open, so I sneak a look, noting the name plate. 'BEN AMBROSE, CEO'.

His head is down and his face is full of concentration. His features are angular and defined and, without his usual smile, his brows are furrowed. He looks almost annoyed. I just want to take a moment to look at him. His sleeves are rolled up and tight around the muscles of his arms, his hair is all messy perfection. I think I have fallen hard for this man. I knock on the big wooden door and wait for an answer.

"Yes!" he shouts out. It's not like a booming boss voice, more a *How can I help you* tone. I inch the door open, peaking in, then put my head around it as he looks up from his laptop.

"Hi!" I say softly. It takes a few seconds for the recognition to hit his face and he smiles broadly, those blue eyes staring back. He straightens up and moves swiftly around his desk to meet me.

"Hi yourself," he says in that smooth Scottish tone. I open the door wider and step into the room. "I didn't expect to see you!"

"And that's why I'm here. No expectations."

I walk further into his office and have a look around. It's modern and functional. A big desk at one end and a sofa seating area with coffee table to the side. Before I can take any more in, he's with me and I'm enveloped in his arms. He smells as amazing as always, warm and spicy. I close my eyes as I take in the feel of him. He pulls back slightly to kiss me on the lips. It's soft and sparks fly through my body.

He looks at me as if I am but an apparition or that I'll bolt at any minute. "Have we got much time?"

"Not really, it's a fleeting visit. I do need to head back to Sammy, I've given her a bit of space. I just needed to see you."

"Do you want to head back to mine for a coffee or something to eat?"

"What about your work? I don't want to disturb you."

"I'd rather be with you than looking at spreadsheets!"

"To be fair, I'd rather do anything than look at spreadsheets."

"It's not far, I can drive us over and drop you back at Sammy's."

"I have the car, but I can follow."

"Not a chance. I want to spend every last second I can with you." He turns back, grabs his laptop and phone and takes my hand as he goes towards the door.

We arrive at an old Victorian building that doesn't look like much, hidden away down an unimposing street. We park in a secure covered car park and make our way to the front entrance. There are two big wooden doors with no numbers, just an intercom to the side. He uses his key fob to enter and as the doors open it unveils an interior that is unexpected. There's a security desk with a uniformed man concentrating on the screens in front of him. Ben gives him a salute as he walks past, which is answered with a brief nod, like some kind of code is passing between them.

We enter Ben's flat through another big wooden door with a silver number six on the front. The place is light and airy even from the hallway, with a big open living area to the left and double doors that are propped open. The light is coming from the two huge sash windows that take up a large part of one wall.

The place has Victorian grandeur, with wooden parquet flooring, high ceilings and a big ornate fireplace. I look round in awe, it's really not what I expected. I expected an ultra modern lads' pad, but this has the right mix of old and new.

The walls are a dark navy with bits of modern art work on big canvases. The sofa is all chunky cushions and looks uber squishy and comfortable, dappled with grey tartan scatter cushions. I'm trying to take it all in when Ben calls from further down the hallway. "Would you like a drink? Coffee? Tea?"

I follow the direction of his voice and find him in a modern-looking kitchen. There's an island in the middle with a large bendy tap and sink in the middle. It has a wine shelf with bottles placed inside. There are two breakfast bar stools. The units are a wood colour that match the flooring and hide all the functional part of the place. I hope he doesn't ask me to get the milk out because I wouldn't know where to start.

"So, drink?"

"Yes please, tea would be great."

"What do you think of the place? You've been very quiet."

"I'm just taking it all in. It's not really what I expected."

"What did you expect?"

"I dunno, something more modern I suppose."

"I like old buildings with the high ceilings and big windows. I like a bit of natural light. Well okay, this place has a lot of natural light."

I look up to the ceiling and it has what I suspect are the original cornices and ceiling rose.

"Do you want to see the bedrooms?" I raise my eyebrows.

"You know I can't stay long."

"I know, no shenanigans!"

"No, but I am curious. There's more than one bedroom?"

"Yes, technically three, a master, a guest bedroom and one I have as an office." He directs me through another hallway. "Here is the office," he says, opening the door to a big mahogany desk with a monitor and keyboard, but not much else. We move down to the next door. "The guest bedroom." This room has light grey walls, a king-sized bed in the middle with plain sheets, and a fluffy sheepskin rug on the floor. He turns to a room opposite. "The bathroom." It's modern with a double shower wet room at one end, a sink and toilet at the other and in the middle is a stand-alone bath. "Down the bottom is the master with en-suite. Excuse any mess, I wasn't expecting company and my cleaner comes during the week."

He opens the door and the room is filled with light from two more huge windows, the dark grey walls don't look so imposing with the brightness. In the centre is a huge bed, crumpled with unmade sheets and cushions on the floor. "Is this where you bring all your women?" I say with a laugh.

"Until now, the only woman I have had in this bedroom is Mandy."

"Mandy?"

"My cleaner!" He sounds a bit annoyed. "I told you, my playboy days are well and truly over. But I get the feeling you don't believe me."

He stares at me for a while and I really don't know what to say to him. I can't just put my insecurities away. He gives me a little smile as if reading my mind. How does he do that? "And for that, maybe I won't show you my amazing closet." He laughs at my quizzical face. "Okay I will. Follow me."

He rounds the side of the bed as if to step behind it, but what I thought was an alcove is actually the entrance to a big closet, fitted from floor to ceiling with racks and a large, long mirror to the side.

"Wow! This is amazing! But I wouldn't need one like this, I don't have many nice clothes and my mucky pumps would look out of place."

He laughs. "Let's get that cuppa," he says, as he takes my hand and leads me back to the kitchen.

We settle down on the sofa and before I can get comfortable he lifts under my knees and moves me so my legs are on his lap, my back to the armrest. "I want to look at your face while we talk."

"That sounds like it is going to be a serious talk."

"Maybe. There was something you said in Paris that I wanted to ask you about."

"Okay, what was it?"

"You said you couldn't get pregnant."

"Ah. No I can't. Is that going to be a problem?"

"Not to me."

"Not to me because what? You don't want kids with me or you don't see us being that serious?"

"I am serious about you Emma. And I haven't wanted to have kids."

"You say that now, but in two or three years' time, you might change your mind and that's something I can't give you. You are a young man and I can understand you might want to start a family."

"Listen, I didn't exactly have great parental role models. So it's never been something I have really wanted." He looks down at his cup of coffee. "I feel like this is another barrier that you are putting up."

"I'm sorry. I'm just trying to be realistic."

"Start by telling me why you can't have more kids. Is it solely because you don't want to have anymore?"

"Partly that, but also because I had two traumatic pregnancies. Some people breeze through pregnancy and glow, I just vomited permanently. And when I had Noah, I nearly bled to death."

"Wow that must have been really frightening." He has started to stroke my knee, it's something I notice he does when I'm telling him something hard.

"It was, but even if they hadn't advised me not to have any more children, I probably wouldn't anyway because parenting is hard. Sometimes a real struggle."

"Yeah, I get that, just think of how my Nan felt, lumbered with me to bring up on her own after already raising her own kids. She should have got a medal." He looks at me again. "I don't want us to fight about this, but these barriers you keep putting up, are they because you don't see a future with me?"

"It's not that I don't see a future. I haven't even looked. I'm just a realist and I have to know that we are both in this for the right reasons. I haven't got it in me to invest in a relationship, just to have my heart broken. And sometimes I wonder why you are with me, sometimes I wonder if it would be best for you to be with someone young and fertile that can give you everything you want."

"But all I want is you. All your baggage, your kids, your insecurities. I want them all, if I haven't already pointed this out to you. I am falling for you, and there's nothing I can do to stop that."

"Really?"

"Really!" He leans over me to kiss me but then moves back to pull my legs down the sofa, so I am flat on my back. I can't help giving out a little squeal. He crawls over me until he is nestled in between my thighs and his mouth is only a fraction away from mine.

He looks into my eyes like he's seeing into my soul and then lands a kiss that takes my breath away. He deepens the kiss like he is desperate for me. Pulling away he says, "Do you want me to show you how much?" He grinds into me, through our clothes and my body starts to throb with anticipation.

We kiss again, hands roaming over each other like we are desperate for the skin to skin sensation. My senses are all over the place, but I hear something in the background. I pull away from him to try and decipher what it is, and then I realise. It's my phone and I push him to let me up and answer it.

"You have got to be fucking kidding me!" My brows knit together as I take in his frustration. He should realise by now that this comes with the territory.

"It might be important." He huffs like a stroppy teenager and moves to let me search for my bag. I get to it too late and rummage around the bottom and pull the phone out. Missed call from Sammy.

"It's Sammy. I need to ring her." Ben has gone quiet, but the look of thunder on his face says it all. "You knew this was part of the deal," I bite. "I told you time was limited." My frustrated tone has him rethinking his simmering outburst. I dial the number and put the phone to my ear, turning my back on him. If this doesn't prove my point about him resenting me, I don't know what will.

"Hey. you okay?" I hear the sobs down the phone before she speaks.

"Hey. Do you think you could pick me up a few things on your way back?"

"Of course I can my lovely. Just message me what you need."

"I haven't interrupted anything have I?"

"No, not really." I turn to look at Ben and he's sitting on the sofa, elbows on his knees and head in hands. "I won't be long." I say before hanging up.

I wait until he looks up. "I have to go."

"Right." He blows out a breath.

"Don't be pissy with me."

"I'm sorry. It's just frustrating."

"Can you take me back to my car please?" The clipped tone makes him realise I don't appreciate his attitude.

"Don't be upset with me."

"I shouldn't have come." I feel really emotional, I wish I hadn't been right about my divided time being an issue. I feel like I may burst into tears. I'm sad that our time was cut short, but we knew it would be. I'm more upset about Ben's reaction.

"Don't say that!" He stands and moves towards me, enveloping me in his arms so that I can't move. "It was just the timing, not the interruption. I know we are on borrowed time, and I've loved that you've taken time to see me, however short it has been." My body begins to relax in his arms and I move to be able to hug him back.

But there's an undercurrent there, of how things will be later down the line. Is he going to react the same way if my children ring, my friends, work?

Ben grabs his keys and we head to the door.

Chapter Twenty-Six

It's Sunday morning, and it's been a rough night. It wasn't really the events that were tough, because we didn't do much, but it was seeing my best friend upset and in discomfort. Then there was the aftermath of emotions that were playing on my mind. I didn't want to tell Sammy because she would have blamed herself. So, I decided the best course of action would be to distract both of us before I leave.

I head into her bedroom with a cup of coffee. "Hey sleepy head, how you doing?" She's already awake and shuffles herself to sit upright in bed.

"Same as ever. I'll feel better after this." She takes the coffee, takes a sip and groans as if it is the best thing she has ever tasted.

"Well I have got a plan for today that will cheer you up."

"Do tell!"

"Well I thought we could head out to watch some rugby."

She looks at me with a quizzical expression and then smiles. "Oooh muddy men in tight shorts, yes please!" I knew that would spark her interest. She always had a thing for rugby men too. "What made you think of that?"

"Well I may or may not have been inspired by knowing that Ben will be playing today."

"Ah, that explains it."

"But I may need your mate's help getting all the info. I don't want Ben to suspect we are coming."

"My mate?"

"I know you lot have been in cahoots with Piers. I'm not daft!"

"Okay, you've got me there. We have been catching up over coffee a few times. He really is a top bloke. Heart of gold and is looking out for his friend, as am I." I roll my eyes.

"Right, send him a message and then jump in the shower."

Here we are, standing next to a muddy pitch, sunglasses on, arms linked together to keep the wind off us, watching a load of buff men wrestling each other and dive through mud. Although the sun is out now, it's been a particularly wet few days and the pitch and the players can testify to that.

We haven't been here long, and we made sure we arrived after kick-off, so Ben wouldn't see us. I didn't want to put him off, but I also wanted to see him *au natural*, in the wild, so to speak. That may have been a bad idea. He's made some hard tackles, but he's taken some too. He's completely covered in mud already.

Sammy is ogling all the players, in their striped jerseys, tight shorts hugging muscular legs, but I can only see one player. "Did you tell him why you are here?" she asks without looking at me.

"No. He knows I'm here to support you, but that's all. It's got nothing to do with anyone else."

"Thanks. I would have understood if you needed to tell him."

"I don't need to justify my actions to anyone," I say with a little bit of venom that shouldn't have been directed to her.

"That's my girl," she says, without turning her head. I smile. "Is it bad that I'm enjoying seeing Ben get pounded?" I laugh at the change of subject.

About five minutes before half time he spots us and points. I blow him a kiss and his face lights up with a broad smile, just before he gets taken down. Once he gets back up, the level of aggression in his game has been dialled down. When the whistle goes, he jogs over to us.

"Well this is unexpected." He looks between us. "Two visits in two days. You are spoiling me." There is no hint of sarcasm and he leans forward to plant a kiss on my lips.

"I brought Sammy to see her favourite show," I say with a laugh. "Don't you need to get back to your half time team talk?" I point to the rest of his team who are looking over. Sammy gives them all a flirty little wave.

"Yes probably, and I'll definitely get the piss taken out of me now. Just watch how much more I'll get tackled in the second half."

"Sorry, not sorry!"

He laughs then gets serious. "Are you staying until the end?"

"Not sure, we do need to get back."

"Can you just stay until I get changed?" He looks at Sammy. "Maybe I can introduce you to some of my team mates." He knows that would definitely make her want to stay.

"Maybe! I'd like to meet them too."

He brings his gaze back to me and narrows his eyes as he jogs backwards towards his team. "YOU are not meeting them, YOU are mine!"

As the final whistle blows we walk back to the club house to wait for them. He was right in his assumption that his game would get harder. The rest of the team, in cahoots with the opposition, made Ben's game as difficult as possible. He must be completely battered. Every time they tackled him to the ground or body slammed him, they would wave in our direction or wink at us. They have really made him pay for having us watch, but Ben is taking it in good spirits.

He walks into the bar dressed in a shirt and club tie, smelling absolutely delicious, no trace of all that mud from the pitch.

"Hey," he says as he gets close. He puts his arm around my waist and looks down at me. He plants a quick kiss on my lips.

"They really took it out on you after they saw us, didn't they. Are you okay?"

"I'm fine, but I'm gonna feel it tomorrow. They always give me grief for being a part-timer. You being here was an added incentive." He looks away "Alright Sammy?" He lets me go and directs his words to her. "Can I introduce you to some friends?"

A few of the guys have gathered behind him. "Guys this is Sammy and this," he points to me, "is my girlfriend, Emma!" I give him a wide eyed look of shock as he introduces them all by name but I'm so taken aback by his introduction that I don't take a single one in.

Sammy shakes their hands. "Maybe you ought to have told her she was your girlfriend first?" says one of the boys. "Nice to meet you, Emma!" I smile back as he shakes my hand.

"Maybe!" Ben says , and laughs.

"We can't stay long," I say. It seems like that's all I've said to him in the past few days.

"I've not scared you off have I?" He steers me away from the others and lets Sammy chat.

"No, it just came as a surprise that's all. But we do need to get going. I've been away from home for a while and I can feel tension brewing."

"Okay!" He looks at me with a smile, trying to find the words. "Thanks for coming. I've loved seeing you."

I smile back. "I've loved seeing you too..." I give him a big smile and he wraps his arms around me. "Boyfriend!" I say and roll my eyes. He laughs and pulls me in for a kiss.

I smooth my hands up his body, wrap my arms around his neck and pull him into another kiss. I break away and slip out of his hold to make my way over to his group of friends. "Come on Sammy, put the nice men down!" She smiles. "We've got to go!" She nods and says her goodbyes and we make our way out of the clubhouse.

Chapter
Twenty-Seven

As I pull into the driveway I see a familiar figure sitting on the doorstep. I stop the car and get out, pull my bag out of the boot and make my way to the door.

"I didn't expect to see you here! I'm not at home you know," I say with a little laugh.

"I know, I knocked." Beth's face is sad. "I just needed somewhere to go." I look at her quizzically.

"You have my spare key, why didn't you just let yourself in?" She shrugs. "Want a cuppa?"

We both head into the house and I click the kettle on. We get settled on the sofa with our cups of tea before I ask her what's going on.

Beth looks really down, her face not the usual ray of sunshine. "I stormed out of the house in a massive strop!" she explains.

"I've been gone an hour and a half and no one has even noticed. He's not even rang to see whether I'm dead or not."

"Oh! What did they do? Or should I say what didn't they do?"

"They just never bloody listen." She sighs again. "I'm now just feeling sorry for myself. Of course he'll say that I'm all emotional, and *I'm probably on my period*." She uses air speech marks and a mocking tone for the last part. "He forgets the fact that I was just reacting to the dumb shit they do!"

"I totally get it. Remember I have lived with three men! You can just hang out here for a bit. I'm not much company though, I'm shattered."

We start to chat but before we can go into any other detail, a noise comes from the front door. I stand up and check out the commotion. The door is wide open and there is a stampede of feet going up the stairs, while David stands in the doorway with a face like thunder.

"Welcome home boys!" I shout up the stairs with a roll of my eyes. David stands in front of me arms folded.

"Is there anything you'd like to tell me?"

"Like what?" I answer as abruptly as the question is asked.

"Well, are you seeing someone?" he says through gritted teeth. I'm wondering how he could have found out, but also why it has anything to do with him. Beth wanders through to the front door.

"I'd better get off, leave you to it!" She heads past David who only makes the slightest of movements to let her past. She turns to me after she passes, making the sign of a phone to her ear and mouths *call me!* I give her a brief nod and focus back on David.

"What if I am? Why has it got anything to do with you?"

"It's got everything to do with me because it affects OUR children." I'm not quite sure which direction this conversation is going, because the boys have had nothing to do with Ben. He continues anyway, like he always does. It wouldn't have mattered what my answer was. "Did you realise it is effecting our children? When you are parading men about in front of them."

"Firstly, how is it affecting them? They don't even know him. And I'm hardly parading him around, he's never even stayed here."

"Well the boys have told me that BEN..." he spits his name out with venom, "has been distracting you and they don't like him. They feel like you're neglecting them, constantly on the phone with him instead of being with them and fobbing them off on your friends so you can hook up."

Wow that really cut deep into the mummy guilt. They never said anything about Ben before. I know that he popped over while he was *in the area* – a very likely story – and I wasn't in. Joshua had answered, and they had a bit of a chat, that's all. I had a go at Ben for popping over unannounced. I was annoyed with him. If I wanted to introduce them, I would do it on my own terms

I don't want David dictating my personal life, but if it is affecting the boys then I can't have that. "They didn't want to say anything to you because they don't think you will listen." I'm shocked by his words. When did I become the parent who wouldn't listen?

"What is someone with a flashy car and money doing with someone like you? What could he possibly see in a forty-year-old mum who has let herself go?" I am completely taken aback by his statement and it really stings, mainly because it just confirms everything I have already thought. "He'll get bored of you soon enough, and then you will have upset our boys for nothing."

"I think you better leave." Tears pool in my eyes. I move forward gesturing him to move out of the still-open door.

"You better sort this shit out Emma!" I close the door in his face. He storms off down the drive way and I hear his car leaving.

I slide down onto the floor, back against the wall, and the tears start flowing.

I wait about 30 minutes to compose myself before I ring Ben. I just need to get this over and done with. He answers in one ring. "Hi Princess. Missing me already?"

"Hi…" I had thought about what I was going to say for ages, going through my words in my head over and over again. But as soon as I hear his voice, it all goes out of the window. I'm wondering if I'm being rash, then David's words hit me full on in the face again. "I'm sorry, I can't see you anymore!"

"Very funny!" He laughs, then composes himself when I don't answer. His tone changes to deadly serious. "Emma? What's going on? What's happened?"

"I just…"

"Emma?"

"The kids are struggling with me and you." I can only say short sentences for the fear of bursting into tears again.

"You mean David has found out and he's giving you grief!"

"He says the kids are finding me too distracted."

"He's manipulating you?"

"Whether he is or he isn't, I need to put my children first. And I told you that you would start to resent me if our time together was impacted. And I saw that in your reaction yesterday."

"Please don't do this! I..."

"I'm sorry, I have to go." I hang up before he can say anymore and now the sobs come thick and fast. I manage to pick myself up off the floor and head to the kitchen, but the thought of food turns my stomach and I suddenly feel nauseous. I plonk myself on the sofa, put the TV on for some background noise and sob into a cushion so the boys don't hear anything.

I think I cried myself to sleep and I'm suddenly woken up, still on the sofa with a wet cushion. I look at the clock – it's been about two hours I've sat here as sad as anything. I hear a banging on the door. That's what must have woken me up. I wish I could just ignore it, but that's just not me. I pull myself up, straighten myself off and head to the door, hoping it's not David for round two.

I open it to a stricken looking face. "Ben! What are you doing here?"

"I thought this conversation should be face to face."

"I can't do this!" I say, shaking my head.

"You definitely can't do it on the doorstep. Can I come in?"

I turn around and head back into the living room, leaving the door open so he can follow. "I don't know what you want me to say?"

"Well you can tell me why you've done a 180 on us in the space of a few hours."

I sigh and start to explain. "The boys have been telling David that they don't like our relationship, and that I'm distracted because of you and effectively neglecting them."

"You know that's not true, right? He's just jealous and trying to manipulate you."

"Even if there's a hint of them not being okay with this, I have to end it. It's not fair on them."

"And have you asked the boys about it?"

"They told David because they didn't think I'd listen."

"Convenient!"

Before the conversation can go on any further there is a commotion at the front door and in barrels David looking unbelievably agitated. His face is red and his hand are clenched in fists by his side. He's like a man possessed. "What the fucking hell are you doing here? GET OUT!" he spits at Ben.

"I could be saying the same thing as you, barging in here like you own the place," I say back to him. He turns on me, his chest rising and falling like he can't get enough air, his face all screwed up.

"And you!" He points his finger at my face. "Your erratic behaviour is affecting OUR children. You just hook up with some random bloke that gives you half a look and you open your legs for him!"

At this, Ben stands between the both of us, facing him down. "Back the fuck off! Don't speak to her like that!"

"I'll speak to her however I like, she's MY wife!"

"Not any more, mate!"

I pull Ben back before he does something he'll regret. "Please just leave it!" There's a thunder of feet down the stairs and the boys clamber into the room.

"We heard shouting." Noah looks between us all.

"Sorry boys, we're just having a chat." I try to shield them from this car crash, like I always have done.

"While they're here, why don't you ask them?" Ben gestures towards the boys, glancing back at me.

"Leave them out of this!" David replies.

"Ask us what?" asks Joshua.

"Well your Dad here says that you are unhappy with me seeing your Mum."

"Who the hell are you to be talking to my kids? Just get the fuck out!" says David, completely ignoring Josh and Noah.

"This has nothing to do with how the children feel about the situation and everything about you wanting to continue to manipulate Emma," he spits back at David.

"We are fine with it. Mum seems loads happier. And he's okay, I guess." Joshua is speaking directly to his father, but David is acting as if he hasn't said a word. He just continues to seethe at Ben. Out of the corner of my eye I can see Noah making a phone call. I need to shut this down straight away.

"Let's just calm this down. Ben, I think you should go."

"I don't want to leave you here with him acting like this."

"Just go!" I shout at him. I need to do anything to get him out, because him being here is just going to cause David to flip out even more.

"Find someone more your type and age," David says to him before he turns back to me. "He's undermining me in front of my kids, and you're parading him around like you're some fucking cougar. Don't flatter yourself. You're nothing special."

I'm holding Ben back again, putting myself between both men. I can see Joshua getting more and more angry. Whether it's because his opinion, that his father so wanted to get across, is being ignored, or at the venom towards his mother, I don't know.

He suddenly explodes at David. "Don't you fucking talk to my mother like that. You have no right to come in here and dictate to everyone and disrespect her." I'm a bit taken aback by his statement. By him standing up for me.

"How dare you speak to me like that," he spits at Josh and turn turns to me. "Is this how you have taught them to act?" He points at me and then raises his hand as if to hit me. In a flash, before anyone registers what is happening, Joshua has punched his father in the face. David staggers back holding his nose. We all fall silent. We are all in shock.

After what seems like an age, but is probably a minute, Lizzie and her ex-partner Jonathan pile through the door. They take a few moments to survey the scene. Jonathan is in the Police. I have no idea what he does to be honest, but he does have that air of authority about him.

He looks at Ben. "I've got a good mind to arrest you for assault. What the hell has happened?" Ben puts his hands up in surrender, seemingly taking responsibility while David still holds his face, blood seeping through his fingers.

"It wasn't him, it was me!" Joshua says, still looking full of anger. "And you should be arresting him." He points over to his father. "For threatening and coercive behaviour toward my

Mum." Jonathan looks over to Lizzie and a silent conversation passes between them.

"Boys, go and grab anything you need for this evening and wait at the door." They both leave while Jonathan, hands on hips, weighs up both men.

"Ben, I think you should go," I say, breaking the silence.

"I don't want to leave you like this."

"Well, you'll have to. I've made my feelings clear and I need you to leave."

"Emma?"

"Ben! Look, why don't you go out with someone more suited to you... like Ami!" The venom that comes out with that statement is not necessary. But he could be with anyone and I'm too complicated. I don't want to drag him into all my shit!

He just looks at me. He doesn't answer and I am starting to sound exasperated. I wish things were different and, in another world, I would be keeping Ben and kicking everyone else out. But I must think of my children. Plus, he has overstepped the mark and started to push me into doing what he wants, even if it's ideally what I want too, and I know he's right.

"I don't need to be manipulated by two men, thank you!" I gesture to the door. Ben looks horrified. That he has been put in the same league as David. He turns and leaves, passing the boys in silence.

Jonathan looks at David. "Don't do anything fucking stupid." He then turns his attention away from him. "Two minutes Liz!" He walks to the door and indicates to the boys to leave, but pulls back Joshua. "You don't solve things through violence. You could have been arrested." He says this loud enough for us all to hear. Then he leans in to whisper to Josh, and shakes his hand before returning back to the room.

The boys leave and he turns his attention back to David. "This is what's gonna happen. I'm gonna walk you to your car. You are not gonna say a word. Then you will drive home and not return here until you are invited back." He waits for a response. "Do I make myself clear?"

David starts to move towards the door. "Why am I the one in the wrong?" He's obviously feeling brave and wants to get the last word. "She's the one who is fucking every bloke that gives her the time of day!"

"Shut your fucking mouth or I'll finish what Josh started!" Jonathan replies without a flicker.

"I'm staying!" Lizzie states. It's not a request.

"I just want to be on my own!" I say to her, tears ready to make a comeback.

"Tough shit!" The front door closes and I crumble onto the sofa. Lizzie heads off to make some tea.

"You gonna fill me in?" she says over the noise of the kettle.

"I think you got the gist!"

"How come Ben was here?"

"David told me the boys were feeling neglected. And other stuff about how Ben would probably get bored of a 40 year old mum who has let herself go... his words not mine!" I take a deep breath. "I called it off with Ben. Next thing I know he's at the door begging me not to break it off and in walks David... The rest, I think you can deduce." I think about how it escalated. David came back very quickly after Ben got here, like he was waiting for him.

"Okay, what I don't understand is how David found out." I shrug. "We'll circle back to that one later. But also why you broke it off with Ben on Dickhead's say so?"

"Because he pushed all my buttons. And when I spoke to Ben, he effectively told me I was being manipulated…"

"Which you were."

"I know. But I just can't deal with the back and forth. Them constantly biting at one another through me. It's just not worth it. I don't want to spend my time refereeing a bloke's pissing match."

"But you really like him. We can all see he makes you happier. Doesn't that count for anything?"

"I'm just being realistic. There's also the distance and the fact that Ben will resent the time I need to have with other people as opposed to him."

"I thought it would have been Ben that decked him though!" She does a little laugh.

"It seems that Josh picks up a lot more than we think. David went for me, I was already holding Ben back and Josh just snapped. I really don't know how to handle this situation. I can't condone anyone's actions." I think for a minute. "Anyway, how are you here?"

"Noah called for back-up!"

"And how come you two turned up together? It's not Jon's week for the kids."

"Well… That's a story for another time. He'll have words with Josh about appropriate behaviour."

"I'd like it to be a story for now. It would definitely take my mind of this shit show."

"He was at mine when Noah called."

"And why was he at yours?"

She lets out a long breath. "It's complicated... and I don't really know what's going on myself, to be honest."

"Are you two back together."

"Noooo!" The word is drawn out and there is an expression of something I can't quite put my finger on. "We did hook up though. I don't know how it happened and we've been spending more time together. And you know we get on!"

"That's nice though. Look Liz, why don't you head off? I just need to be on my own."

"I can't leave you!" The conversation is interrupted by the sound of Lizzie's phone. "Saved by the bell! She stands up as she answers the phone. She moves away from me into the kitchen, but I can still hear her side of the conversation.

"Hiya... She's as okay as she can be... She doesn't want me to stay... Well, I know that!... I'll tell her but she's not going to like it... Right okay... See you in a bit." She hangs up the phone.

"What am I not going to like?"

She gives me a look. "Jon wants someone to stay with you tonight. The locks need changing and he doesn't want you here on your own if either of them decide to come back tonight. And I have to agree with him."

"I just want to be on my own for a bit, get my head together." I look at her with a pained expression.

"I know that. But he said he'll come over, sleep on the sofa, keep out of your way. You know he's a man of very few words. He doesn't like to talk about feelings and what not, so you'll be safe. And he only uses his interrogation skills on the bad guys."

She does have a point and I know if Jonathan is offering to sleep on my sofa, he has a genuine concern. Before I know what's going on there's a knock at the door. "That'll be him. I'll leave you to it and we'll talk more tomorrow." She gives me a quick hug and makes her way to the door. I hear them have a brief conversation and then Jonathan comes in.

"You okay?" he asks, warily. I'm not sure whether he is worried about me biting his head off for coming over, or having some kind of emotional outburst.

"Yeah," I say. He looks relieved. "You could have one of the boys' beds rather than the sofa you know."

"No, I'd rather be down here. Nearer to the door in case... Well, you know!"

"Right," I say. "I'll get you some bedding, then I'll head to bed." I leave him in the living room, gather together some sheets and pillows, and dump them on the sofa. I head to bed without another word.

I manage to put my pyjamas on in some kind of auto pilot mode and get into bed. I pull the cover over my head and squash my face into the pillow as the tears break free again. I sob until I fall asleep.

Chapter

Twenty-Eight

Ben

I don't remember the drive home. I remember pulling up outside a shop and buying a big bottle of non-descript rum. I made my way through the lobby of my building and told Mike, the security guard, that I didn't want any visitors or deliveries for the next few days. He gave me a sad nod, my face probably told him exactly how I was feeling.

I don't remember much of Sunday night either. I texted Sean to tell him I was taking some time off and wouldn't be in next week. In reply I got a barrage of messages, which meant I had to tell him that Emma had dumped me.

I messaged Mandy to tell her not to bother cleaning this week, because I didn't want to make any pleasantries, I just wanted to wallow.

I went to turn my phone off, but then decided it would be a good idea to look through my photo gallery. And there she was! There were photos of Emma, of the two of us from the night we met, right the way through our stay in Paris and the night I gatecrashed their night out. I just couldn't stop looking at them. Over and over again, the pain in my chest getting increasingly hard to ignore, each time.

I put my phone on flight mode so I wouldn't get any messages, and in a way, to stop me from messaging Emma, begging her to reconsider, telling her how much I loved her or to check that she's okay. I know she will be okay because she has her group of friends around her.

I started my drink with ice, and then just kept pouring more drink on top each time the spicy liquid ran low. It wasn't until I was halfway through the bottle that I realised what I was doing. That's when the silent tears started to flow.

I don't remember what happened after that. But now I'm trying to open my eyes and the bright light from the windows stings them. There is a pain searing all over my head, but that is no match for the pain in my heart when I remember what happened yesterday. I sit up, taking in my surroundings. I must have been laid on the sofa, fully clothed, for hours. The rum bottle on the table is empty.

There's a pain in my chest that won't go away. Like indigestion but worse. Nothing seems to ease it. The alcohol just changes the sensation. I feel like my insides have been pulled out and I'm just left with an empty husk. Everyday tasks like eating and washing feel pointless. I'm in some kind of no-mans land, between lives and my body doesn't feel like my own.

I pull myself up and head to the kitchen to get a glass of water. Walking down the hall, I try not to fall over my own feet, I'm clearly still drunk. Once in the bedroom, I close the door and put myself to bed.

Chapter Twenty-Nine

Emma

It's Monday morning after a night of sobbing into my pillow. I have called in sick to work, which they weren't happy about because I already had time off the week before. The boys stayed at Lizzie's last night, so I called the school to let them know they were both ill.

Jonathan is awake and drinking coffee when I come downstairs. He doesn't look well rested, much the same as me.

"Hey!" I say, as I head to the kitchen for a shot of caffeine.

"Hey! Sleep okay?"

"Nope. You?"

"Nope!" Like lizzie said, he's a man of few words. "I rang a locksmith. He'll be round before 10am, and then I will leave you to it."

"Thanks."

"Liz will bring the boys over, once it's done. She didn't send them to school."

"Yes, she messaged, and I rang the school." We need to have a family chat once they get back.

I've been mulling over how this whole situation is going to resolve itself. How we are all going to move forward, especially the boys and their dad. I just have no answers. As far as Ben is concerned, I keep flip flopping backwards and forwards on whether I did the right thing. I generally keep coming back to the fact that I did. In the back of my mind there is still that one massive barrier of distance. I know people do the whole long-distance relationship, but I bet that's not with all the stuff I have going on too.

The way he was when Sammy interrupted our time together just cemented the fact that he would become resentful towards my situation. I can't just drop everything to go to Edinburgh on a whim. And I'm pretty sure he's not going to want to hang out with me and the boys in our little house. Not to mention the lack of sound proofing or locks on the doors. That could become very embarrassing, very quickly.

There's a knock at the door. A feeling of fear washes from my head to my feet. I hadn't realised that the thought of David coming back had affected me so much. Jonathan answers the door to a large, tattooed man carrying a tool box, and my body breathes a sigh of relief.

Once the locks are changed, Jonathan stands with me at the door holding out the new keys. "You'll need to cut some new keys for the boys. Do you want me to do that for you?"

"No I'm fine. I'll go later today."

He holds my shoulders and looks me straight in the eye. "If you need anything, please call me."

"Okay!"

He doesn't move his hand from my shoulder. "I mean it. Because I know you'll try and muddle through by yourself, but don't." I nod and he lets go. He roots around in his pocket and pulls out a card which he hands to me. "If David comes around for anything, ring me. If I don't answer, ring me at work. I'll send the lads round." He winks and gives me a big smile before opening the door and heading out.

"Bye!" I wave before shutting the door.

About 20 minutes later there's the familiar sound of kids at the door. They are knocking and making a fuss as they realise their keys don't work. I rush to let them in.

"Hi guys! Are you both okay?" I try to fuss over Joshua but he's a lot bigger than me and he just shrugs me off. Noah, however, wraps his arms around me and gives me a big squeeze.

"Our keys didn't work," Joshua says, abruptly. I can tell he's anxious. His shoulders are near his ears and his tone is clipped.

"I know. Come on in and we'll have a chat." He rolls his eyes and wanders into the dining space, plonking himself down at the table. In contrast, Noah looks like he hasn't got a care in the world. They both wait at the table. One looks like he's going to his execution, the other to a party. These kids are like chalk and cheese.

"Is this the bit where I get told off for hitting dad?" Joshua bites out and he folds his arms across his chest. He may be all bravado, but his eyes betray him.

"No Joshua. This is not lecture time. I wanted to have a grown-up talk with you both." Joshua relaxes visibly. "I want us to talk through things that have happened, without anyone getting upset, because some of the problems we have right now are through lack of communication."

"Can I get a drink?"

"Yes Noah, be quick!"

"What about a snack?"

"Whatever!"

"Is this going to take long?"

"If you keep asking stupid questions, then it's never going to be over." Joshua says, rolling his eyes.

"Be quick Noah."

Finally, everyone is sat down. "Where do you want to start?" I ask.

"I dunno, maybe at why Dad is a massive prick?" Joshua, as usual, is straight to the point.

"I don't even know where to begin there." I think for a minute. "What did you say to your dad about Ben."

Joshua pulls a face. "Okay, so I may have made things a bit worse than they should have been. See, he was going on ridiculous, rooting through all your stuff. He looked like he was going to have a fit or something. He found some cards and asked if you were seeing anybody. Of course, I wasn't going to tell him anything. It's none of his business." He makes another face, this time with his sorry eyes. "But then he started spouting all this shit and I just kinda spat out that you had a boyfriend and he was rich and awesome and that."

"But you don't even know Ben."

"He doesn't know that. Then Noah told him his name."

Noah looks scared, like he's in trouble. "How did you know about Ben, Noah?"

"Well I've heard you on the phone with him, and your phone flashes up with his name." Now I'm really glad I changed his contact name on my phone from *Love Of Your Life*, that would have taken some explaining.

"You said he was awesome and your dad translated that into you were upset and didn't like him? Typical of your father, that."

"I know. And when he lied about it in front of me and then ignored what I had to say I got mad. Then when he was saying all those crappy things to you. I just lost it."

"Josh, this is where I need to tell you that violence is never the answer." He rolls his eyes. "But also how much I appreciate you stepping in and defending me."

"I just don't get it." He is starting to get angry again. "Why do you let him treat you like that? All those times he's talked down to you, made fun of you or just not listened to what you had to say. I'm bloody sick of it." He takes a few breaths. "Not to mention the way he talks down to us too."

"Okay, just take a breath. I'm here to listen and I'm sorry I didn't before."

"You know this whole thing was just a massive power trip. He wants to go off and do his own thing, but also wants to have this power over you. He saw Ben as a threat and he used us to get to you the best way he knew."

"That's very perceptive of you. I didn't think you paid that much attention."

"I have hidden depths." Joshua smiles at me.

"Mum?"

"Yes Noah." I'm expecting some random question that has nothing to do with what we are talking about.

"Do you love Ben?" The question has caught me so off guard, I'm not sure what to say. Tears threaten to fall again, and I don't know if I can be honest with my children. Or even with myself for that matter.

"I don't know." I pause. I need to be open with my children about my life, my feelings. "I think I might, yes." Noah does an excited little squirm in his seat. "But we are not together anymore."

"Why not? If you love him?"

"It's complicated."

Joshua turns to Noah to speak to him directly. "That's what adults say when they don't want to tell you the reasons."

Now it's my turn to roll my eyes. "Okay then." I take a deep breath, giving me a little bit more time to figure it out. "He lives far away and I have a lot of things going on. I just don't have the time to be going up and down the country. And he runs a business and works long hours."

"So?" Joshua shrugs.

"So! Having a relationship is hard work. And I think we would both get mad at each other for not being able to spend time together."

"Better than being mad at each other when you are together."

"I know, but he's going to want different things from me eventually. I don't want to end up a few years from now being really sad."

"You'd just rather be sad now then." Joshua shakes his head. "You know he was gonna take the blame for me hitting Dad. I bet if I hadn't said anything, he would have done time for me."

"Bit dramatic Josh!" I say.

"So we'll not get to see him again? I kinda liked him." Noah looks sad.

"You never even spoke to him Noah. AND you're a rubbish judge of character."

"Okay, let's forget about Ben for now. What would you think about me going out on dates and seeing people? In general, I mean."

"I don't see it's any of our business, just like it wasn't Dad's."

"I think it will be nice. You have seemed really happy. And you've stopped wearing those leggings with the holes in." Thanks for that Noah.

"Change of subject. What are we going to do about your father? As you know I've changed the locks so he no longer has a key. I'll get you both a new one, but I need the old ones back." Both boys fidget and get their old keys and throw them into the middle of the table.

"I don't want to see him again. He's an arsehole!" Joshua says folding his arms across his chest.

"You know what they say, if you have nothing nice to say, don't say anything at all."

"I want to see him. I don't understand why you both hate him." Noah sounds sad.

"We don't hate him."

"Dad is being horrible to Mum." Joshua starts. "He doesn't really give a shit about us. Haven't you noticed how many times he cancels seeing us? And when we go over to his, he still has no time for us." Now I'm getting an insight into what happens when the boys stay there. "He's too busy with work, or whatever girlfriend he has at the time. Think about it Noah, when was the last time that Dad asked about what you were interested in?"

"I don't remember."

"How many times have you told him that you don't like mushrooms on your pizza, and how many times has he ignored you and got one with mushrooms on?"

"Every time we get pizza!" Now it is being explained to Noah, he is starting to understand.

"You know how Jacob and Sienna's Dad takes them bowling, and has them every other week, for a whole week?"

"Yes."

"How many times does our Dad take us out to do things like that?"

"He took us to that funday last year."

"That was for his work, and what did he do at that funday? He hung around with people he worked with and gave us money and told us to get on with it. Out of the two hours we spent there, he was with us for a total of 15 minutes."

"Well, that's not kind." Noah seems to be voicing his thoughts.

"Okay," I say, turning my attention to Noah. "If you could do anything with your Dad, like a day out, what would it be?"

"I don't know, maybe go karting!"

"I think, rather than not seeing him, maybe you could put together some kind of rules and things you want to do while you're together." They both shrug.

"I think we need to talk about how things work here too. I can't keep doing everything for you. You both need to be more independent. We also need to communicate more. Maybe we should have at least one meal together, here at the table, to talk about our week. We can draw up a list of jobs that need to be done and look through who does them and when."

"Sounds fun..." Joshua states, sarcastically.

"Oh can I draw up a list?" Noah is ever the enthusiast.

"But what about you Mum? What are you gonna change?"

"What do you mean?"

"Well, we are changing the jobs we do, what about you? You've started to dress better at least!" Joshua looks at me with a half-smile, wondering whether he can get away with that comment.

"I wasn't that bad. You think I should change my job?"

"Well you always say you hate your job. You come back grumpy."

"That may have something to do with having to be pulled out to pick you up constantly!"

"Maybe, but is it something you see doing forever?"

"Alright Oprah!"

"Who?"

"Never mind! No I don't see me doing it forever, and I would quite like to get back to what I was taught to do."

"So do it then."

"It's complicated."

"It's not complicated. Look for a job and apply for it. The end."

"Jeez Joshua, who made you the boss?"

Chapter Thirty

Piers

Sitting at my desk I can't quite focus on work today. I stare out of the door waiting for something, anything, to happen. It's an unusually slow day today and I hate those kinds, they drag on. I would rather be ridiculously busy and stressed. I lift my head up to find Jack gesturing through the glass wall of my office, doing a drink motion. I give him the thumbs up and stand to join him in the kitchen.

As I get to the door, my phone starts beeping with multiple messages. I'm about to ignore them and leave, they'll be there once I get back, when it starts ringing. With an eye roll I stroll back to my desk and pick it up.

"Morning!" I already know it's Sean from the caller ID.

"Have you heard from Ben?"

"Erm, no. Why?"

"You know Emma dumped him?"

"I had heard." Of course I'd heard. I'm in constant communication with the girls. Sammy lives near me and we go out for coffee every few weeks. I love them all.

"Well he called off work all last week and no one has heard from him. He's not answering calls and I've been to his flat and his doorman says he's not accepting guests and isn't letting me up."

"Have you asked Ami?"

"No. You're in contact with her. Can you ask? I'm getting worried now."

"Hang on!" I drop Ami a quick message while I'm on with Sean. "If she hasn't seen him, what do you want to do?"

"Hold an intervention!" My phone beeps. "Ami hasn't heard from him either."

"That was quick!"

"Yes, I'm THAT good!"

"Right can you meet me at his flat in 15 minutes?"

"I guess so."

"Right, see you there." I hang up the phone, gather my things and head out the door. I swing by the admin desk and ask Sally to hold my calls and that I'm taking an early lunch. She laughs, she knows I'm not that important.

I'm waiting for Sean outside the building when he comes rushing round the corner looking flustered. He looks concerned and I don't blame him. Ben is generally a bit of a workaholic, so him not being in for over a week is worrying. The only real time he's taken off before was when he took Emma to Paris for a few days. Sean uses his key fob to enter the main part of the building but the light flashes red, so he buzzes for security. The door unlocks and he pushes through.

In the large foyer there's a big security desk and behind it is a familiar face.

"We're here to see Ben Ambrose."

"I've told you before, he's not accepting any guests at the minute."

"I know what you said, but we're really worried about him. Mike, mate, he's just split from his girlfriend and no-one has heard from him."

"Hmm, well he did cancel his cleaner too."

"Surely you need to do a welfare check on him? He could be dead in there for all we know."

"Hang on, I'll give him a call." He picks up his phone to call through the intercom phone up to Ben's flat. No answer. "I'll check CCTV, see if he's left the flat recently." He gets up from his chair and opens the door behind him. He disappears for what seems like hours. When he comes back out he looks between the two of us. "What relationship are you two to Mr Ambrose?"

"Well, we're his best friends."

"What about family?"

"He doesn't have any. We are his family."

"Look, I just need to make sure you're not just anyone." Sean fumbles around in his pocket, pulls out a business card, then some ID. I see what he's doing, so I search for my own and we hand them to him.

"This is who we are. Look on his details. Does he have an emergency contact listed?" I can see the panic in Sean's face. I think if we don't get to check on Ben soon, we'll be calling an ambulance for Sean.

"His emergency contact is a Ms Amelia Prescott." Sean's face drops once again.

I step in. "Well I think this warrants as an emergency. Ring her. She can verify who we are." He looks between us again and picks up the phone.

"Hello, can I speak to Amelia Prescott please?" We listen to the one-sided conversation. "Hi, I have you down as the emergency contact for Mr Ben Ambrose... That is indeed what we want to ascertain. I have two gentlemen here wanting to do a welfare check on him... Yes one does look rather cross, but I wouldn't say that... I'm not sure I would describe the other as cute but dumb-looking either. Yes well... Okay, I will pass on that message. Thank you for your time, Ms Prescott." He looks between the two of us again. "Ms Prescott has authorised you to check on Mr Ambrose. She also wanted me to tell you that she's his emergency contact because he likes her better than you. Her words, not mine." He stands from his seat and sets off up the stairs. We follow behind. I think Sean's conflicting emotions are that of relief he can check on Ben and annoyance that Ami got one up on him.

We stand outside Ben's door, waiting for it to be unlocked. As Mike pushes the door open the smell is a little overwhelming and I start to worry. But it's not a dead body kind of smell. It's more alcohol, old food and the unwashed. Before Mike can announce we are here, Sean pushes past him into the flat, shouting Ben's name. I look into the living room. The blinds are down and the whole place is covered in empty take away cartons, glasses and empty bottles of booze. The TV is on but muted on some national geographic channel, playing a programme about penguins. Sean has gone straight for the bedroom where I can hear some kind of conversation.

"Get up you dickhead, you had us all worried."

"Fuck off!"

"Get the fuck up before I drag you out of bed. You're acting like a love sick puppy. It's pathetic."

"Alright Sean," I interject. "Chill out, we've found him and he's alive." But he completely ignores me and continues at Ben.

"Do you know that we've all been worried about you?"

"Fuck off and leave me alone!"

"Right! I'm ringing Emma. I'll tell her exactly what she's done to you." And in a split second Ben is up and on his feet, out of bed, if not a bit wobbly.

"Don't you fucking dare!"

"Well sort yourself out then! Go and have a fucking shower for a start."

"I should deck you, coming in here like that."

"I'd like to see you try!" With that Ben, with a face like thunder, slopes off to the bathroom.

"Look at the state of this place." Sean looks round the room then heads into the kitchen. "We better take him for some proper food and get this place sorted out." I head over to the intercom and buzz for the security bloke.

"Mike? It's Piers. Ben seems to be alive, but the place is a dump. Do you have his cleaner's number?"

"Well that's good news. I'll sort the cleaner, when do you want her?"

"As soon as she can. Tell her we'll pay double for a quick job. We'll take Ben out and feed him while she's here."

Ben took a 30-minute shower, but he really needed it. He's dressed in some old joggers, t-shirt, baseball cap and old trainers. I see the look he is aiming for, heartbroken, and he's nailed it. We head out and make our way to a café.

It's a small place with only a few well spaced out tables. We find a place and sit down, I gesture to the woman at the counter and ask for three coffees and a menu.

Ben sits fidgeting in his seat, while Sean sits opposite, elbows on the table, staring at him. "What is wrong with you?"

"What do you think is wrong with me? I'm sad. Well no, actually I'm absolutely devasted."

"So you act like this?"

"What do you want me to do? Push all those feelings down and never let anyone in again? Sound familiar?" Sean's jaw tightens, and he shakes his head. I'm not sure what that all means, but these two have history. They've been friends forever. Luckily the tension is broken by the waitress coming over with the coffees.

"I'm not hungry," Ben bites out.

"I don't care. You're gonna eat." Ben crosses his arms over his chest and I can immediately see what a 15-year-old Ambrose would look like. We look over the menu, order some food and sit in silence again.

"It's okay to be sad. You have every right to have all the emotions." I look at him with a sympathetic smile. "Just don't do it on your own. You scared the shit out of us."

"I know we weren't together for long, but she has just consumed me. Every waking minute I think about her. But now instead of it making me smile, I have this pain in my chest." Sean rolls his eyes and I boot him under the table.

"Do you want to tell us what happened?"

"Not really." He blows out a breath as he thinks about what to say. "She rang in tears, said her ex had told her the boys hated me or something and she had to finish it with me. Of course he was talking shit. I didn't even get to answer her really.

"So I got in the car and drove down. When I got there, we didn't get time to talk because her ex just stormed in, throwing all kinds of shit at her. The boys came down, told her what he said was a lie, he got pissy and her boy punched him in the face before I got chance to. Then her mate and, well I don't know who, piled in and she says I have to go, find someone more suited to me." He shakes his head. "...Like Ami? I mean, where did she get that from?" He thinks for a minute. "Oh yeah, and I'm trying to manipulate her too!" He throws his hand up in the air in exasperation, but you can see the hurt in his eyes.

"What now?"

"I wallow in self-pity. Or at least I would if you two would let me."

"What and have you let the business go under, just because you're feeling a bit sad?" Sean is really angry at him and I'm not quite sure why. Our food arrives and we eat in relative silence.

"Soooo." I draw out the word to grab their attention. "What now? You can't go back to wallowing in your flat."

"I know!"

"Well you better pull yourself together because we have those business awards in two weeks and we can't have our CEO looking like he's having a nervous breakdown." Ben glares at Sean. I've never seen the two of them like this before, it's weird. I know Sean doesn't show much in the way of feelings, but this is a bit harsh. Now the role that Ami plays in Ben's life is apparent. She's his emotional support.

I break the tension. "Why don't you focus on work? Keep your mind busy, that will help."

"Maybe."

The food is finished, and the plan is to go our separate ways. Outside the café I give Ben a hug and tell him to stay in touch. They turn to head in the opposite direction, back towards the flat. I'm due back at work, but I watch as they make their way down the street. I can tell by their stiff shoulders and animated hands that they are having an argument. This obviously goes back further.

I set off walking and pull my phone out. I dial the first of two people I need to speak to. The phone rings once. "Cute but dumb looking?"

She laughs loudly. "I didn't say you *were* dumb, you just look it. And I said cute." I roll my eyes even though she can't see. "I take it you rescued him."

"Yes, but he's not great, mentally. And Sean is being a bit of an arse with him."

"Typical. I'll give him a call tonight."

"Thanks Ami, speak soon." I end the call and straight away dial the next one. "Hey, Sammy. How are you doing?"

"Hey Piers, good to hear from you. We haven't had a catch up in a while."

"I know and I'd like to get together after work if that's okay? I need to talk to you about some stuff."

"Tonight?"

"Yeah. And is it possible to get some of the girls on video call too?"

"I take it you don't mean Emma." She knows exactly what this catch up is going to be all about.

Work still hasn't got any busier, which is okay today because I have other things on my mind. As soon as the clock hits 5.30pm I pack my things up and head out the door. But instead of going home I head to the coffee shop that I usually meet Sammy in.

I open the door and an old fashion bell clinks above my head. The place is an old Victorian terrace, not particularly out of place in Edinburgh. It's away from the main streets, so it's not too busy at this time of day. She's already there with her laptop and a coffee. As soon as she sees me walking in she smiles and stands, waiting for me to give her a hug.

"Hey. How are you?" I know that something has been upsetting her. Whatever it was, it was highlighted by Emma's trip to Edinburgh.

"I'm good. You?"

"Same as ever!" I point to the laptop. "You got the other members of the Coven joining us?"

"Cheeky, but yes. Order yourself a coffee and I'll ring them. They are all ready." I stand up head to the counter to order my coffee. I can see her screen on my way back and there's a split screen video call. Megan and Beth sitting together, they look to be at work, and Lizzie from her living room. Sitting down next to Sammy, I peer in.

"Afternoon ladies!"

"I've got to say I'm not one hundred percent at ease with having this conversation behind Emma's back." Sammy is right, but needs must.

"I get it, but I need to tell you all some stuff and then, as her friends, you can decide what she needs to know and what we need to do about it."

"Do I need to be here?" Lizzie is always the reluctant talker and has a look of distain on her face.

"Of course! You were there for the... whatever it was." She rolls her eyes at Sammy.

"Right, I first want to say, I shouldn't be telling you guys any of this, but I am. Can we just be honest in this conversation and hold no allegiances? I think it's safe to say we all want Emma and Ben to be happy, either with or without each other. But if truth be known, I for one think it should be together." Both Beth and Megan nod, Lizzie still has a look of distain, so I continue. "Ben has been AWOL for over a week and we found him today, in a mess, completely shattered. He is heartbroken."

"He's not the only one. Emma has been all quiet at work and been overly productive, which makes the rest of us look bad."

"Do we know why Emma broke it off? I mean, the truth."

"It's complicated," Lizzie pipes up.

"Complicated how?"

Lizzie blows out a breath. "She was really shaken by what happened."

"I can imagine, but that surely had more to do with her ex than with Ben."

Sammy looks at me, then turns back to talk with all of us. "She really likes Ben, I mean properly. But there's several barriers holding her back."

"Which are?"

"Well, David said the boys didn't like Ben, and although that's not the case, I think it planted something in her head."

Lizzie follows on. "Then the fact that she doesn't think she deserves the happiness. She thinks Ben could do better, which we all know is bollocks."

"And the fact that he is younger and might want a family of his own, which she can't and wouldn't want to give him."

Megan sits forward to talk. "I think the biggest issue is distance. She struggles balancing everything as it is, so travelling to Edinburgh, making time for a long distance relationship is almost impossible. Especially now the kids aren't seeing David."

"But other people make it work. It's not that far." My eyebrows knit together at the thought. Does Emma just not want to make the effort. It doesn't seem like her.

"It's a whole different ball game when you have children. It's not the physical distance as such, it's the mental distance. She can't give him all of her emotional time. He'll want her to block the rest of her life out when she's with him and that's just not how it works. Eventually, he'll come to resent her for being emotionally unavailable."

"Wow, this is how women think?" They all laugh, well except Lizzie. "I think what has hit Ben really hard is not being able to fight his corner."

"Yes, but does fight his corner mean trying to emotionally blackmail her into a relationship that she can't see lasting? She's really had enough of that with her ex. And she's only just finding herself again."

"So is there anything we can do? Can we get them to talk at least?"

"How? They can't just bump into each other." Beth shrugs.

"It needs to seem organic and not that we've forced them together."

"Or that he's ambushed her," Lizzie says.

"It has to be something that they both attend independently."

"There's the business awards next month, I know he's going there. His company is nominated for one."

"I think my lot are going to that one. I'll check but I could take her as a plus one." Sammy replies.

"We're going to the Dog and Swan on Friday. If you mention it to her beforehand, we could encourage her to go."

"At least it gives them the opportunity to talk about it, if they want to."

Well that's settled. If it's meant to be they will sort it all out. Now to let the girls do their magic. If nothing else, this conversation has been an eye opener into what women think, and I'm a little bit scared to be honest.

Chapter Thirty-One

Emma

Three weeks later

I took on board what the boys said in our family meeting, and in the spirit of open communication, we have set up a Discord server. Apparently, WhatsApp groups are for old people. Who knew!? I have also decided that, within reason, and in the interest of transparency, I am sharing everything that happens with them. Hopefully they'll understand a bit more about the workings of life in general. To be fair on them, they did completely school me at the last meeting.

I message them.

Me: Boys can you come down, I need your help!

Noah: K

Joshua: K

Since when has Okay been reduced to K? It's not exactly a long word to type out.

Eventually the boys are downstairs, Noah is already sitting at the table. He is revelling in his new responsibilities. The first thing he did was write a list of all the jobs that needed to be done in the house, with only a little prompting. We then sat around the table and shared some of them out. Giving them jobs of cleaning up means that they generally try to avoid making the mess in the first place.

Joshua is the last to take his seat. He is a little less eager.

"What's up Mum?" Noah bounces on his chair. That kid can never keep still.

"Well I have some things I wanted to talk to you about. I have been thinking about money, and with your dad not being in touch, I think we need to prepare for if he stops paying for things."

"Would he do that?" Noah looks glum. His dad is still on a pedestal.

"Yes he would. Just to have another thing to hold over Mum."

Noah wrote to David, outlining what he wanted their relationship to be. That he wanted to spend time together but that he needed him to listen to him, consider him more, and most importantly keep to the arrangements he made. Noah gave him a list of activities and ideas of how he wanted to spend their time together. We posted the letter together so there could be no suggestion that I hadn't posted it, but it's been a few weeks now and we've heard nothing. That in itself has made me anxious about money.

The divorce settlement had David agree to continue paying half of the mortgage, and for it to be the boys' permanent residence, until Noah turns 18. Then the house will be sold and the equity split equally. I'm conscious that he may stop paying that and stop the money he sends me to help with bringing up the boys. And that would be a financial catastrophe for me, so I need to get some steps ahead.

"I've applied for a new job as a Marketing Manager, which pays more than I'm currently on, and it's what I'd like to do as a career, rather than my current job. I got a call to say that I had an interview. The only problem is I haven't had an interview in forever, and I need your help."

"Exciting. Can I ask you questions? Is it like on the apprentice?" Noah squirms again.

"Yes kind of, I suppose." Noah offering is lovely but I have no idea where this will lead.

"Brilliant, I'll need to write some questions."

"Maybe let Josh be in charge of the questions." Who knows what questions Noah will come out with.

"I'll download some," Joshua says, getting his phone out of his pocket.

"We need to make it look like an interview." Noah stands and starts to rearrange the furniture.

After an hour of what I can only describe as interrogation and a load of laughter, I have apparently been successful in gaining employment at Lowther and Sons. I am actually feeling much more relaxed and a little bit more ready for the real thing. I haven't told anyone else about the interview in case it is a disaster.

Chapter Thirty-Two

I'm sitting in the lobby of a tall glass building that houses a number of companies of varying sizes. Continuing as I mean to go on, I have dressed the part. My camel-coloured pleated skirt comes to just below the knee and is matched with a black camisole top and blazer. I had to wear the killer heels that Sammy bought me because they seem to bring me good luck, of sorts. I have a portfolio of designs and ideas ready and my hair is pulled up into a high ponytail. I took a quick selfie and it took all my strength not to send it to Ben, like I would have done before.

Over the past few months I have put on a brave face. The days haven't been too bad. As long as I kept myself busy, and generally didn't make chitchat, I wouldn't have to think about him. The evenings, however, have been awful. Those are the times I'm generally on my own with enough time to analyse everything.

It's also the times he would usually call to see how my day went. And then laying in bed, I think about all the time we have spent together and mull over whether I've done the right thing. I always end up crying into my pillow.

They say time is a healer, but I think every day gets harder, realising that we'll not be together. That the phone won't ring with him asking how my day's been, or just to hear my voice. Or the silly random messages I get.

The first few nights there were some rambling messages that didn't make much sense, but they stopped pretty quickly, and I surprised myself with the feeling of disappointment, even though I didn't reply. The amount of times I have nearly rang his number, just to hear his voice, but it would do neither of us any good.

That train of thought is broken by someone calling my name, it's the receptionist I spoke to when I first arrived. I stand and follow her through some big glass doors.

Once I'm out of the interview I can't recall what was said. It was like some out of body experience. I probably made an idiot of myself. I get tongue tied and try to be funny when I'm nervous. They said they would contact me before the end of the week to let me know if I had been successful. The journey home was mainly trying to piece together what had happened. I can't learn from the experience if I have no recollection.

I open the front door, drop my bags on the floor and slip out of my shoes. The boys must have been waiting for me coming back because I've never seen them come out of their rooms so fast.

"How did it go?" Noah is full of energy as usual.

"When will you find out?"

I answer Noah's question first. "Well I think it went really well." It's only a little white lie, "and I'll know by the end of the week." I walk into the kitchen and put the kettle on, the boys in tow.

"I thought, because you'd had a stressful day, instead of you cooking, we could get a takeaway." Well played Joshua.

"Are you paying?" His face drops. I know he doesn't have the money, it passes through his fingers like water. Noah, on the other hand, has more money than me. Like I say, my kids are like chalk and cheese in many respects.

"I'll pay. I've got some money saved."

"Oh Noah, you don't have to, but I think takeaway is a good idea. What are we having?" The boys discuss the options, but the conversation is soon broken by the ring of my phone. It's a number I don't recognise but answer straight away.

"Ms Lowther? This is Stacey from Noble and Young. I just wanted to contact you to thank you for attending your interview with us today." I put my finger over my lip indicate to the boys that it was important and they go silent in anticipation.

"It was lovely meeting everyone." If they are calling this quickly, it must mean I really messed up the interview.

"We would love to offer you the position of Marketing Manager." I so am stunned I forget to reply. The boys gesture to me to let them know what's being said.

"That's great!" I manage.

"I'll email you all the details. If you could let us know whether you'll be accepting the position by noon on Friday, that would be great."

"I will do. Thank you, Stacey."

"My pleasure. I look forward to hearing from you."

I hang up the phone, look at the boys and try to find the words. I'm shocked to say the least.

"Well?" Joshua breaks the silence.

"I got it!" The boys erupt and start bouncing round the kitchen with whoops of joy. They both fling their arms around me in a hug until I have to pull away to breathe.

Chapter

Thirty-Three

This week has been going pretty well, considering. I accepted the job offer and they sent through all the information I need. I'm a mixture of excited and apprehensive. First thing is to break the news to the girls. We have one of our monthly catch ups at the Dog and Swan. I need to thank Mitch for stepping in last time we were there, and believing me. I have no doubt that given half the chance, that sleazy bloke would have blamed me for all the trouble he caused.

I'm just about ready. The boys have been given their instructions, but they seem to be a lot more reliable lately. I'm more comfortable leaving them on their own, but to be fair, I don't have much choice. While I put on some lipstick, my phone rings beside me. The caller ID says it's Sammy. "Hiya lovely!" I answer.

"How's my favourite person in the whole world?"

"Okay, what do you want?" She always starts a conversation this way if she wants something.

"You see, the thing is... I need your help."

"Oh jeez, what this time?" I laugh.

"Sooooo I have to go to this awards thing next weekend. I need a plus one to keep me sane."

"You could take anyone. I'm sure there's some hotty you've hooked up with that would love to go."

"The thing is, he's going... with his wife!"

"Ah, right! When do you want me to come up?"

"Love you Em!"

"You bloody better. Send me the details cos I'm just heading out to the Dog."

"Will do, have a good time!" I hang up, grab my things and head downstairs. I hear a car beep outside, so I type a quick message to the boys to say I'm leaving. I open the door to see a car waiting for me.

It's early enough to find seats at the Dog and Swan and the girls park themselves around a table. I head off to the bar for the first round, but also to have a word with Mitch. He's busy bottling up a few mixers but I beckon him over. "Hey Mitch."

"Hey Emma. How are you and the girls?"

"We are good. I just wanted to say thanks for not throwing us out last time we were here."

"Why would I have chucked you out? You're my favourite customer." He beams back. "Anyway, you were the victim in it all."

"I know, but Ben was also in the wrong."

"How is Action Man?"

My face falls. "We've split up."

"Not because of what happened?"

"No... it's complicated."

"Well, he's an idiot."

"I'm thinking that might actually be me. Anyway, thanks." He gives me a quizzical look, as if to say, how could I be the idiot.

"No worries. Drinks?"

"Yes please, we'll have our usual assortment of fruity ciders, please."

"Coming right up." He lines the bottles on the bar, I take them over to our table, and return for the glasses.

Once everyone has their drinks and we've all settled down I take a breath to deliver the news. "So girls, I have news." They all sit up straight, ready. I'm not sure what they are expecting to hear.

"I have been offered a new job." There is horror on Beth and Megan's faces for a moment and then the smiles break.

"That's amazing news, you didn't even tell us you had an interview." Lizzie is the first to congratulate me.

"I know, I wasn't sure how it would go, and I didn't fancy telling everyone when it went pear-shaped."

"Well, tell us all about it. Although, can I just tell you I hate you for escaping our office. But I'm also equally proud of you." I knew it would hit Beth the most. We sit opposite each other and she is my work bestie. I don't think I could survive that place without her.

"I put my two week's notice in today. It's a Marketing Managers position with Noble and Young. I'm really excited. The boys encouraged me to go for it. They even helped me practice for my interview. It's very different from what I do now."

"We're so pleased for you." Megan says. "Have you told Sammy?"

"Yes, I told her the other day, I wanted to tell you guys in person."

"How is Sammy? What's going on with her."

"Yeah she's good. She's called today to get me to go to some event with her next week."

"And are you gonna go?"

"Oh yeah. She pulled a guilt trip, so I have to go."

"Does this mean we're gonna have to go clothes shopping again?"

"Oh do we have to?"

"Well yes. You want to look amazing, don't you?"

"I'm not really that bothered, I'm only helping Sammy out. Who have I got to impress?"

"You might meet someone special."

"And look where that got me last time."

A fleeting thought about Ben crosses my mind. He won't be there will he? This isn't some kind of intervention again by my so-called friends. No, they wouldn't do that, surely. I push the thought from my mind and focus back on the conversation.

"Megan has something to tell us!" Beth says, and we all look towards Megan who has a puzzled look on her face.

"Do I?"

"Erm yes. The fact that you received flowers the other day to the office, and they weren't from Darren."

"Are you gonna enlighten us?" Lizzie asks.

"The card said they were from Shelley, but who is Shelley I wonder?"

"Ah." Megan pulls a face like there's a story behind it. "Can I just say, before you go all batshit crazy on me and start planning a wedding, it's not what you think." We are all waiting in anticipation for what she's about to say, and I bet all of us are hoping she's dumping Darren.

"The flowers were from Sean. He is in my phone under Shelley, so I don't get grief about it. Let me reiterate, because I know what you lot are like. There is absolutely nothing romantic going on with him, we just talk about stuff."

We are all looking at Megan in astonishment.

"Well you kept that little nugget quiet," I say.

"Sorry Em! We don't talk about you and Ben, I promise."

"It's fine! Just be careful. Not specifically about Sean, but this could blow up for you."

"I know, I am." I think we are all in stunned silence.

"Well I've got some news too," Lizzie starts and look around the group. She has everyone's attention. "I've been sleeping with my ex!"

"Wow. And are you getting back together?"

"I don't know."

"And how long has this been going on for?"

"A few months."

"How did it all happen?" The interrogation has started. These girls are like vultures, picking away at food once they've started.

"It just kind of happened. We still get on really well. I don't know what will come of it. It is what it is?"

"Why did you split up in the first place?"

"I actually can't really remember, something about work, quality time and both of us *wanting different things*, I think!"

It's turned out to be a night of revelations, and I thought we all led boring lives. I think we need another round of drinks. And pronto.

Chapter Thirty-Four

Ben

This is probably the longest week of my life. Work has been constant yet uneventful. I thought throwing myself into work would help me forget about Emma. It hasn't. It just makes the days seem so much longer and the nights torturous. I miss ringing her after I get home of an evening. And when something has happened, I immediately want to share it with her. But I can't.

Ami has been messaging constantly and although I appreciate her checking in, I don't think I can go through what has happened again, dissecting every last thing I did wrong and every way that Emma rejected me.

Sean is also very little help. He has virtually no empathy about how I am feeling, and zero sympathy. He's been burnt himself and has completely closed himself off. He has made it clear that he thinks I have to do the same and that love inevitably leads to heartbreak, so why bother?

I think the only person I'm prepared to talk to is Piers. He has a softer side than Sean and he's been there for the debrief, so I don't have to go through it all over again. But deep down, the main reason is that he keeps in contact with the girls, and I'll get a little glimpse into Emma's world, even if only the smallest crack.

Pulling my phone out of my pocket, before I change my mind, I message Piers and ask him to meet me for a drink. He answers straight away and I gather my things. As I leave the office I poke my head around Sean's office door. "I'm just going out for a bit. I shouldn't be too long." He just grunts. I have no idea why my whole situation has narked him so much.

I open the door to the bar. It's dark and has a familiar smell of stale beer. It's away from the main streets so doesn't get the tourists the other bars do. Piers sits at the bar waiting for me, two drinks in front of him. He must have headed down as soon as he got my message. "Work that good that you can come for a drink in the middle of the day?"

"Oh yes, its riveting at the minute. You are a welcome distraction." There is no amusement in his face, so I know he isn't joking.

"Yes, well I needed to get away from my desk too."

"So what's up?"

"Same as ever really. But I can't speak to Sean. If I even mention not feeling myself, I get an eye roll."

"What's the craic with him anyway?"

"It's a very long story, and I bet he won't want me sharing it. He'll say it's in the past, but he's been totally closed off ever since." He just nods, knowing not to delve any further. "So have you heard from the girls?" As soon as the words leave my mouth I regret being so straight to the point.

"Is that why we're here?"

"No, I was just making small talk really." A complete lie.

"Okay then. I have heard from them. We chat a bit about everything and nothing." He looks to me, I think he's wondering whether to tell me more. "Emma's got a new job." My heart stops even at the mention of her name. I want to ask a hundred questions. I want to text her congratulations. But I can't. I think for a minute about the best response.

"That's great news." I try to sound unaffected, but I'm not sure it worked.

"What've you got coming up with work then?" He's changed the subject quickly and I'm annoyed and grateful at the same time.

"Not a lot really. Well there probably is, but I can't quite get my head in gear."

"Are you going to those Business Awards next week?"

"I didn't know you knew about those."

"Sean mentioned it," he says, rather too quickly.

"Yes, we have been nominated for a sustainability award, or something. But... I don't know. I'm not sure I want to go. I just can't be bothered socialising at the minute."

An unrecognisable flicker crosses his face that I can't quite read. "Don't you need to be there? Ami may need a plus one too."

There is something afoot here. "Is Ami going?"

"She said she was. You can't leave her to manage all those arseholes by herself."

"She's a big girl, she can handle anything." He looks down at his drink and the conversation stalls.

"Do you think you'll see Emma again?"

That's thrown me a little bit, but I have thought about it often. I want, more than anything, to see her again. "I don't see how I would. It's not like I will bump into her in the street, or in a bar." And then something in my head makes the connection. I would bump into her if, say, she was with Sammy. "Is Sammy going to the awards?"

He looks sheepish. Piers can't lie for anything. It's written all over his face. "I don't know, she never said." I bet she has. "If you saw her again, what would you say to her?"

"Who? Emma? Can't say I've really thought about it." Another lie, it's pretty much all I think about. What I could say differently, what I could do differently. If I just got another chance. Maybe the way this conversation is going, that might be a possibility. "I mean what could I say? I don't really know what went wrong." But Piers obviously does if he has been in communication with the girls.

"Maybe it was just distance after all." Bingo, he does know what's going on. I pretty much came to the same conclusion.

If you strip everything back, it all comes down to distance. She thinks she has too much on her plate to commit to a long-distance relationship, and also that I would resent her not taking time to spend with me. She may be right there because I did want her whole attention and that was selfish. There was also the thing about me wanting kids. She didn't seem convinced that I didn't want children of my own. And I really am not bothered about it either way.

"Maybe." My mind is going ten to the dozen. If I do see Emma, then what would I say to her? Where do I start? If the only thing that's standing in the way of us being together is distance, surely I need to make plans to close that distance.

I take my phone out of my pocket and look at the blank screen, "Ah sorry mate, that's Sean. I need to get back to the office." I know I have lied to him again, but he'll forgive me for this one.

But Sean is going to be really pissed with what I have to tell him. I jump down from my seat and grab Piers in a big hug. He's not expecting it and nearly falls off his chair. His face is a picture. He has no idea what's just happened. I rush out of the door and back to the office.

Chapter Thirty-Five

Emma

News of my new job has spread like wild fire in the office. Literally anyone who walks through the door has interrogated me about it. When I handed my resignation into my boss, slight relief passed over his face. It seems the firm hasn't been doing so well, so one less person to pay is a god send.

There has been a not-so-secret collection for a leaving present. Not-so-secret because it's Beth that's managing it. Sitting opposite her, I see everyone coming and going to her desk and the whispers. Although I am as nervous as ever about my new job, I really can't wait to get out of this place. It represents the old me and I really need to move on from that.

There's still no sign of David. I contemplated getting in touch with some of his friends, but I didn't really want to see him either. It's just the money uncertainty that's worrying me and also that Noah is desperate to speak to him. He's got it in his head that his Dad isn't speaking to him because of the letter he sent. I told him he's probably away with work and hasn't got the letter yet. But it's been weeks now.

Megan and Beth dragged me round the shops again looking for the perfect dress for this thing I'm going to with Sammy. I don't see what all the fuss is about. They were even going on ridiculous about the underwear that I needed to go with it. No one is going to be looking at my underwear, but they insist that *you never know*, and it gives the dress a better flow or something.

The organisation of this trip has gone far more smoothly than I had anticipated. Lizzie suggested she come over and stay with the boys. Her kids are with their dad, but they are going to get together and maybe go out for the day.

The train journey up has been quite relaxing. Much better than driving. I've been able to read my book and eat a sandwich in relative peace. It's a welcome change because I feel like I've been running around all over the place this last week. Trying to tie up loose ends at work and preparing for my new job at the same time. I jumped into a cab straight outside the station and I've made my way to Sammy's.

I buzz the intercom and there's a crackling on the other end. "It's me, let me in." The lock buzzes and I push my way through and up to her floor. I knock on the door and Sammy inches it open looking panicked. "What happened to your face?"

"Is it that noticeable?"

"It's bright orange."

"I had a bit of a mishap with the fake tan."

"Just a bit?"

"I've been Googling how to fix it."

"I think we're past fixing it and more onto the covering it up. Are you gonna let me in?" She opens the door further and rushes back to the living room.

"Argh!" She scrolls through her phone while I go to switch the kettle on. "It says here that you can make a DIY paste to reduce the effects."

"Okay, and what are the ingredients?"

"Baking soda, oil and lemon juice."

"Do you have all of those in?"

"No!"

"Which ones do you have?"

"Oil. Possibly, I think."

"Well then that's a no. Also, putting lemon juice and baking soda on your face is a recipe for disaster. Won't it burn your skin? Joshua would know."

"What am I going to do?"

"Have you got baby wipes?" She looks clueless. "Baby oil?" She shakes her head. "Oil based lube?" I'm clutching at straws now.

"Oh I definitely have lube, but I don't think its oil based."

"Massage oil?"

"Oh yes, I'll go and get it." She heads to the bathroom and comes back with a little bottle.

"Lay down, head on the arm of the sofa." I get a towel and some cotton wool pads. I lift her head and place the towel underneath. I place a pad on each eye, because knowing our luck, she'd get oil in her eyes and then it would be a trip to accident and emergency. I gently rub the oil into her face. I have no idea if this will make any difference or not. "How did this happen anyway."

"I put it on and then got a phone call. I forgot I had it on." I start to remove the oil with the cotton balls and I think it's starting to get a shade lighter.

"Well if this doesn't work, at least you've had a relaxing face massage." I wipe off the last of the residue and hand her the mirror. "It's made a bit of a difference."

"Has it though?"

"Well yes. You've gone from neon to tangerine."

"That's not funny."

"We'll cover it with make-up. It'll be fine." She makes a huffing noise but seems resigned to fact this is now a cover-up mission. "So, what do you need to tell me about tonight?"

She sits up quickly, a shocked look on her face. "What do you mean?"

I eye her suspiciously. "Like, who do we need to avoid, who we need to be nice to? Just the usual." She relaxes a bit, what did she think I meant? "What are our code words if we see your man and his wife?"

"Oh right, well how about just use his name, or initials at least? JP and wifey. As for the others, I'll point them out. There are definitely some very handsy blokes I work with you'll need to avoid."

The door buzzes. "Are you expecting someone else."

"Yes, food. I ordered some Chinese for us before we get ready. There's a meal at this event, but I intend to have had a few to drink by the time that comes out." She stands up and goes to open the front door. "I thought we could have some now, but not too much that I don't fit into my dress, and then we have some for when we get home."

"Good plan!" I start to open the food while Sammy gets the plates.

An hour later and I'm smoothing down the front of my lace dress. The food was much needed, but it's made the dress a little tighter. I opted for as classy black lace dress. It's quite low cut and the scalloped edges of the lace are a contrast to the fair skin of my cleavage. There's little capped sleeves and it clings to my curves all the way down to the floor, with a split up one leg, or I'd not be able to walk. And of course, my lucky heels. My hair is wavy and pulled off my face at one side with an elegant diamond slide.

I walk into the living room where Sammy is opening a bottle of fizz. She looks up. "Wow, you look amazing."

"So do you." Sammy is wearing a navy velvet dress with cowl neck and dipped back. We certainly do scrub up well. "What's the fizz for?" She pours two flutes out and hands one to me.

"I thought we could have a toast."

"Okay, what to?"

"I don't know. A future of happiness."

"Okay, to a future of happiness." We clink glasses then take a drink. After a few mouthfuls and a bit of giggling, Sammy's phone buzzes to tell us the taxi is outside. We gather our things and head out.

We arrive at the venue. It's a majestic old hotel in the centre of Edinburgh. The foyer has a stone floor which makes our shoes click-clack as we walk. The event is being held in the ballroom and we follow the signs. We walk through a bar and seated area that is almost deserted, and through the big double doors.

The room is decorated for the event with round tables towards the staged area, which could probably seat about 200 people. The bar area is separate and spreads along the length of the room. It's bustling with people chatting to each other.

Waiters pass by with trays overflowing with champagne glasses full of the amber liquid. Sammy grabs two at the first opportunity. I nod over to an easel which has a seating plan on and we head over to check out where we are sitting.

I feel him before I see him, the hairs stand up on the back of my neck and a shiver runs down my back. I whip myself around to see him standing with a group of people, chatting away. He's wearing a navy three-piece suit, with a tie only barely visible. I've never seen him looking so good. His angled jaw and his slightly messy, uncomplicated hair. He looks a bit thinner, but still the same firm, sharp physique.

A wave of anxiety hits me, and I can feel the flush of it from the top of my head to the tingle in my toes. I'm not even sure why I'm feeling this way. I didn't give Ben much opportunity to fight back when I told him it was over. Maybe I think he'll call me out on my bullshit reasons in front of everyone. Is it just the sight of him, releasing all those feelings I've spent the last month pushing down and trying not to acknowledge?

I turn back and focus my eyes on the board, double checking that my mind isn't playing tricks on me. I scan the seating plan, and there it is. A whole table designated to Ambrose Holdings. "Did you know he'd be here?"

"Erm..."

"Sammy!" I'm starting to have a little panic. What do I do, what do I say? Do I just avoid him for the whole night, or do I leave? "Did you set this up so I would see him?"

"No. Well kind of. It wasn't just me."

"Who else then?" She looks to her shoes and I know straight away. "So everyone has had a hand in this then?" She nods but she can't make eye contact with me. "Did he know I was coming?"

"I don't think so. It was Piers who made sure he was coming. He's been nominated for an award, so there was a very high possibility that he'd be here."

"For fuck's sake. You're meant to be my friend and you kept this from me."

"I did it for your own good. You've been miserable, and I don't think either of you has had closure. If nothing else comes of it, at least you could part on better terms."

I huff out a breath and turn to look at the group again. He's spotted me and gives me a small smile. I look back at Sammy. "I need to leave."

"Emma no, Please!"

I'm so conflicted. I down my drink thinking it will give me a bit more clarity, but it doesn't. My heart is racing, my chest burning. I feel panicked, but I realise it's not because I didn't want to see him. It's because I miss him and I so desperately want to be with him. I thought if I had no contact all the feelings would just disappear. But here I am, a complete mess from being in the same room as him.

Some of Sammy's colleagues have joined us and are introducing themselves, unaware of the absolute torment going through my mind. I know they are talking away, but it's as if they are over the other side of the room. "I'm going to the toilet. Get me another drink," I say in Sammy's ear and she nods.

I excuse myself and head to the ladies' room. I need a bit of space to process seeing Ben. It's been about a month now, but the pull towards him hasn't dulled. I don't know what it is about him. I have been able to think rationally about our split, until I saw him. There is something not the same about him though, His eyes don't shine like they did, and his smile doesn't reach as far.

I stare at my reflection in the mirror wondering what the hell I am doing here and how I'm going to manage the rest of the night knowing he is only a few metres away. My heart aches at the thought of not being with him, but it's not something I can think about because the barriers are there, no matter how much we might want it.

I hear the door opening and I turn to see a strikingly beautiful woman walk in, she's tall, blonde and slim. I turn back to the mirror to reapply some lipstick, if only to hide the fact I'm having a minor meltdown.

I presumed she had gone into a cubicle but out of the corner of my eye I can see her standing, looking at me. "Emma?"

"Yes!" I look towards her trying to work out who she might be.

"Hi, I'm Ami."

"Of course you are!" I eye roll, I knew Ben was lying when he said she was nothing special. I should have guessed all along. And by the look of her, he would be better off being with her.

"Can we talk?"

"Why?"

"I want to talk to you about Ben."

"There's nothing to talk about."

"I think there is," she says firmly, as if starting to get irritated with me.

"Look! I'm no competition for you. I'm not going to stand in your way with him."

"Emma, you've got me all wrong."

"Have I?" I am being really curt with her.

"Ben is in bits about your break up. I'm just his friend and I'm worried about him. We're not romantically involved." She pushes each cubicle door to see if they are empty, but one is occupied. "Can we go somewhere to talk in private? I don't want this aired in public." She stands outside the occupied cubicle and kicks the door. "Aye Tiff?" And there's a little squeal from inside.

"Okay. But I'm not sure it's going to change anything."

She gestures to the door and I follow her out. But instead of heading back to the ballroom we go out to the foyer bar that is practically deserted. "Drink?" she asks.

"I think I'll need one. Gin please, large!"

She heads to the bar and I sit at one of the small round tables. After a few minutes she comes back with two drinks and places them on the table. She looks at me, trying to find the words. "I can see why it may look like there's something going on between us, but I can assure you there isn't.

"He helps me out at these functions. It's not easy for a successful woman at these things. If I have a handsome man on my arm, the gropey brigade stay away." I muffle a little snort. I can see how it must be a problem for her. "Ben is not my type."

"Ben is everyone's type!"

"You are more my type than he is."

I look at her for a moment trying to process her words and then the realisation drops. "You're gay?" She nods. "But if you tell people you prefer women, won't that stop men hitting on you?"

"Quite the opposite. I'm then classed as a challenge. I obviously haven't had a real man blah blah." She rolls her eyes. "...Can I watch? ...You know where I'm coming from." She sighs.

"Yeah absolutely, I get it!"

"Back to Ben. He's absolutely devastated."

"I don't know what you want me to say." I shrug.

"He said your kids were upset and you didn't think the distance would work."

"Well the boys are fine. It kicked off with their dad and he lied that they were upset."

"So that's no longer a problem then."

"It's more complicated than that." I sigh and she's waiting for more. "I have my kids, my job and I don't get much time of my own. He would just resent me for not being available. Maybe not at first, but eventually."

"That's a shame. I honestly don't know whether he'll come out of this."

"Don't!" I say curtly.

"Sorry, but I've never seen him so happy, invested, besotted and then so devastated."

"Well it's not easy for me either." I try to stop the sob from coming out.

"You do have feelings for him then?"

"I'm not having this conversation with you. I don't even know you." I take a big drink. I wait a moment, but there's nothing left to say so I stand and walk back into the ballroom.

I spot Sammy sitting at our table and weave around all the chairs to plonk myself on the seat next to her. "Why did you bring me here?" This is all getting a bit too much, I'm not sure how long I can hold it all together.

"What's happened?"

"I've been given the guilt trip."

"By whom?"

"Ami."

"His date?"

"Yes, but it's not as bad as it looks. He's not her type." She pulled a face, questioning my words. "*I'm* more her type. Her words, not mine!"

"So that barrier has now been blown up."

"That wasn't really a barrier, more an annoyance."

There's a clattering of plates as the food is being served around us and both our attentions are drawn to the people on our table we make pleasant chit chat. None of them knows the turmoil that's going on in my head.

Chapter Thirty-Six

Ben

I saw her as soon as she entered the room. As did every male in the place. She looked absolutely stunning, her hair pulled off her shoulder to show off her neck. The lace of her dress follows every amazing curve of her body. She walked in elegant and graceful, even in her favourite stilettos. I couldn't take my eyes off her, but I needed to pull my attention away.

Since I picked up on the intervention by the girls and Piers, I've been trying to sort my head out. What would I say to her, how can I make this work? Then trying to come to terms with the unthinkable, that Emma doesn't feel the same way about me. I've had a month without her and it hasn't got any easier. The ache in my chest has only got bigger. Sometimes I feel like my heart will just stop.

I've talked to Sean about what I intend to do. He isn't happy about it, but when I told him I couldn't function the way we were going, I think he got the message.

I keep looking over at her. She's looking at the table plan. I've worked out where both tables are and once everyone is seated I will manoeuvre myself to sit in her line of sight. She looks over and catches me staring at her. I give a little smile and I can tell from her body language that she had no idea that I was going to be here.

She says something to Sammy and rushes out of the room. I put my drink down, attempting to follow her, when a hand on my arm holds me back. "I need to go." I say to Ami.

"No, you'll just spook her. Let me go." I watch Ami head out of the room and I don't know how I'll contain myself until they come back.

I make small talk with all kinds of people, but I'm not all there. Half of my brain is wondering where she is and hoping that Ami doesn't make the situation worse. We start to filter into the main part of the room and take our seats. I'm hoping Emma hasn't just given up and gone home. Hers is the only seat left empty at the table. I switch seats so I'm facing her, but the panic is growing bigger the longer the seat remains empty.

Just as they are about to serve food, a very rattled Emma walks in and virtually throws herself into her seat and starts, what I have recognised as, a quiet rant to Sammy.

Ami comes and joins us at the table. "Well?"

"Well what?"

I roll my eyes. She knows exactly what. "What was said?"

"I told her we weren't romantically together."

"And?"

"And I told her why."

"You didn't have to do that."

"I think I did. She basically said I could have you."

"Shit, that's not a good sign."

"She still loves you."

"Did she say that?"

"Not in so many words. She said the break hadn't been easy for her either. And then she walked out."

I look over to her again and she's picking at her food. I don't think she's eaten any. Her facial expression shows that her brain is working overtime again. I'll give her a bit of time to process what has happened with Ami.

Once the plates are cleared away the lights go down and the presentation starts. I keep looking over to Emma. She only catches me a few times and I give her a little smile. She is a lot more relaxed now and has even laughed at something that the table has been talking about. But as she chats to a man beside her, my anxiety levels start to rise.

There have been a few awards already handed out, but I'm not really paying attention. I pull out my phone and send her a message. I see her reach for her bag on the table and pull her phone out to read it. Her eyes look up to meet mine. Then she puts the phone on the table. I message again. "Can we go somewhere and talk?" But she doesn't pick up the phone to check it. So I send more. "Please", "Just outside in the bar". Other than standing up and going over all I can do is wait, not very patiently.

Chapter Thirty-Seven

Emma

The lights dim, signaling the start of the ceremony. Ben's table isn't that close but somehow he is in my line of sight. I'm not paying much attention to the awards. Maybe five have been presented but I'm distracted. John next to me has been filling me in on the who's who for each one and I chat politely. Every now and again I look up to find Ben staring at me.

Sammy leans over and shows me the list of awards and nominees. She points out one category – Sustainability Project. It's one of the last awards.

I feel a vibration from my bag and root inside to pull out my phone.

Ben: Hi

I put the phone back down on the table and ignore it. It buzzes again and then again but I resist the urge to pick it up. Then I look up and catch Ben's eyes again. He lifts his phone and points as an instruction to pick up my phone. So I do.

Ben: Can we go somewhere and talk?

Ben: Please

Ben: Just outside in the bar

Me: Why?

Ben: Please

Me: What else is there to say?

Ben: Lots!

I look up and see him stand and leave the room, a scowl on his face. Sean is asking him to stay with a thunderous look on his face. I turn to Sammy and tell her I'm getting some air.

I stand and follow Ben out into the empty bar area. He's waiting for me at the bar.

"Hi"

"Hi yourself." He takes a moment to look at me. "You look amazing."

"You too." And he really does. Up close he is the most gorgeous man I know. But now I'm nearer I can tell that he has been struggling. There are black marks under his eyes and his face has lost depth.

"How are you?"

"Good."

"I heard you got a new job. Congratulations!"

"Yes. Are we just having a catch up here or is there a point to this. I don't think there's any more we can add to what we've already said."

"I haven't even started. I feel that I haven't been able to say anything so far." I just shrug. "You know our friends talk." I nod. "So I know about what David said about the boys wasn't true."

"Yes. Do you want me to admit you were right? That I had been manipulated again."

"No!"

"What do you want to say then?"

"I want to say... I love you Emma."

I blow out a breath. "But it's not enough though is it? To just love each other." I can see the frustration in his face.

"Emma! For Fuck's sake!" He holds me by the shoulders, as if he's going to shake some sense into me. But he just looks at me with that cross, beautiful face. "Can you just open that bloody door and say *Hello Happiness* and welcome the fucker in?"

"Are you marking yourself as *Happiness* in this metaphor?"

"No I'm not. But I'll help you open that door. I'll even prop the fucking door open for you!" He's exasperated. But nothing has changed. "Just please give us a chance... At happiness."

"But there are still barriers. The door is well and truly locked and nobody has the key."

"We'll find the fucking key. What exactly are the barriers that are left? As far as I can see they are all gone."

"Except one!" My heart sinks, I've been over it in my head, again and again.

"Tell me what it is. Tell me what to do. I will do anything it takes."

"Anything?"

"Anything!"

"Even move your whole life, your company, your home down to me?"

"Yes!"

My heart actually stops and it takes a few moments to breathe again. I mustn't have got that right. "Yes? Just like that?"

"Not just like that. This isn't just a spur of the moment thing to win you back. I've thought about it, looked into things. I've looked at moving the company, I've searched for homes for us, the four of us."

"Wait what?"

"Emma! I NEED you. And it's clear that you don't need me. But do you want me? A life with me?"

I feel like my head is about to explode and I can't quite take in air, think rationally or speak. "I can see this may be a bit too much to take in right now. Maybe you should process what I've said to you and give me your answer by the end of the night." I nod and make my way back into the ballroom. I have no idea what just happened.

I sit next to Sammy. My face must be a picture because she picks up on it straight away. "Bloody hell, what happened?" Without a second thought, all the words come out of my mouth in one long trail. I'm surprised she can understand any of it.

Chapter Thirty-Eight

Ben

I sit back down at my seat. It would have been perfect if she could have just accepted everything and said yes, but she needs time to process everything. To be fair I did throw everything at her. I watch as she tells Sammy what's happened, and I can see in her face she's processing it all.

I'm apprehensive about her answer. I don't know how I will cope if she says no. I keep looking up at her and her face tells me she's thinking about it. At least that's something. She catches me watching and I smile. She doesn't smile back, but she picks up her drink and drains the glass.

There are only two awards left. Everything is coming to a close and I haven't had an answer. My phone vibrates in my pocket with a message to meet her outside. When I look up, she's already gone. I try to leave without anyone noticing.

As I go through the door, I can see her standing near the bar again, her back to me so I have no idea what's coming next. My heart starts racing and I feel like I may vomit, right here. As I reach for her, she turns to face me. Her face still giving nothing away.

"So, I've thought about it." A long pause. "And... there's a lot of things to sort out."

"I know." Then a voice from the ballroom shouts over.

"Ben they are calling our award." It's Sean and he doesn't sound too happy. I can hear the murmur of the room as he holds the door open. I put my finger up to indicate for him to give me a minute.

"But yes!" She says and it takes a few seconds to register.

"Yes, you want to be with me?" She nods and a smile spreads across her face. My legs nearly give way, but instead of collapsing I scoop her up in my arms. I never want to let go, but I drop her back down to the floor. I wrap my hand round her jaw and move down to kiss her lips. As I deepen the kiss I hear the faint announcement of Ambrose Holdings.

"Ben!" Sean shouts from the door. "We've won! You need to come back in."

Nothing quite registers fully until Emma pulls away. "Ben you won!"

"I know." I smile down at her.

"I mean the award. Go back in there and collect it." It takes a few seconds to realise what she means so I turn to head back inside, firmly holding onto her hand so she can't change her mind and make a run for it.

I leave Emma with Ami. "Look after her!" I say as I make my way to join my team on stage. My face is beaming and everyone must think it's because of this award. But I couldn't care less.

I mumble through a quick thank you speech and head back to the table. I grab Emma's hand and kiss it, then without taking my eyes off her, I speak to Ami. "Ami, can you tell Sammy we've gone home."

Without waiting for an answer, I pull Emma through the ballroom and out of the door. I stop in the bar area and turn to Emma. "I can't wait to spend the rest of my life with you."

She smiles. "Me too!" I bend down and kiss her.

I pull away after a few moments and bend to grab Emma by the thighs and lift her over my shoulder, fireman's lift style. She squeals as I head to the exit.

"We, Ms Lowther, have a lot of making up to do."

Epilogue

Two Years Later

So much has happened since we decided to give happiness a chance. Not long after Ben made the decision to move south, he found a house for the four of us, enough room for us all to have our own space, friends could visit and that our bedroom was far far away from the boys! I sold the old house and split the proceeds with David.

It just held too many memories, both good and bad. We wanted a fresh start and have as little to do with ex as possible.

I wanted to use the money as a deposit for the new house, but Ben wouldn't hear of it and told me to put it in a high interest account and keep it as an escape fund. I keep joking that I'm using it as a cocktail fund.

The new house is beautiful, full of light and space for everyone. We have extra rooms for the Edinburgh contingent to visit on a regular basis and a home office for Ben. He also set up a satellite office, not far from us, that any of them can work from and took on more property nearby to develop.

The boys have grown into lovely young men. Noah is 15 and has been doing work experience in Ben's company, and Joshua is getting ready to go to university in Edinburgh. He has it in his head that he's going to be living in Ben's posh flat, but I think it would be trashed in a matter of weeks.

In a bigger turn of events, our family of four has turned into a five with the addition of beautiful Ava. She truly was a big surprise to us both. I had stated in no uncertain terms that I would never be able to have any more children, and Ben was okay with that. But I knew he wouldn't always feel the same and a few years down the line he would come to resent me when he changed his mind.

But out of the blue we were contacted by an old flame of his, who had found out she was pregnant a few years before and had kept it from him. As you can imagine, all hell broke loose, and we all rushed up to Edinburgh. Charlotte, Ava's mum, is lovely. She hadn't known how to handle the whole situation with Ben, so she tried to keep him out of the picture. That was until Ava was rushed to hospital and she felt guilty. She had thought Ben might want to *do the right thing,* if she told him she was pregnant, and she didn't want a relationship with him.

Once everything calmed, Ava and Charlotte settled into our life really well. Now I don't even get to be the jealous stepmother. Ava spreads her time between her two families pretty much equally, and we do all the big stuff together. I get all the good things about having Ava and none of the daily complications of having a young child. And I am glad I didn't have to go through childbirth again. I get to play, laugh and be the fun parent, all of which I missed with my boys, having to be mother and father.

It kind of all fell into place. Ben got the child he would have eventually craved, and I didn't have to be a parent again, well maybe just a step-parent.

Along with our friends, we are a massively dysfunctional family unit and we love it. Our boys absolutely adore Ava. She has them wrapped round her little finger. It's going to get interesting when she's older and gets boyfriends who will have to come up against three father figures.

There's still a lot of back and forth to Edinburgh for Ben, what with work and picking up Ava, but he always comes home to me and that's what matters. As Ava gets bigger and starts school full time, there will have to be some changes and we need to think about where we will live.

Joshua and Noah don't see too much of their Dad. Only on special occasions or when he wants to impress people. They keep him and his toxic behavior at arm's length, which also means I don't have to have any contact.

As for me, the new job isn't so new now. Applying for that position at Noble and Young was absolutely the best thing I could have done. When I started, they told me that although I hadn't had much experience within the industry, I had the life experience that the rest of the twenty-something team members didn't. So, I'm mothering them too. I've climbed up the corporate ladder and I'm Executive Marketing Manager and get to build lots of exciting marketing campaigns.

As for my motley crew of friends, they are all amazing and we are still having our monthly night outs at the Dog and Swan. It may not seem like your typical happy-ever-after, but it is perfect for me.

THE END

Or is it?.... If you would like to see what happened next, please keep reading....

Afterword

T hanks for reading my book, I hope you enjoyed it.

But its doesn't have to end just yet. If you would like a copy of the Bonus Epilogue, sign up for my newsletter from this link and a copy will be emailed to you.

Visit carriemcgovern.com/HappinessBonus

Hello Mr Beckett is the next book in the series. Find out what life has in store for Megan and the rest of the gang.

If you would like to follow updates on my work, my social media pages can be found on my website.

Visit www.carriemcgovern.com/socials

Acknowledgements

There are loads of people to thank who have been on this journey with me. Thanks to my friends and family who have supported me and put up with my constant talk about *The Book*. Thanks to Emma and Marian my first Beta Readers, Helen for being a very patient editor, Lauren for being so great with changes to my artwork.

I want to thank my author mentor TL Swan, who from the love of reading her books, helped me write my own. Without you, this book would never have been written. But also to her writers group, Cygnets, without you guys for support, this book would never have been published.

About the Author

Carrie McGovern

C arrie is a contemporary romance author based in the UK. She writes relatable fiction with strong female characters. Her books have a strong emphasis on friendship and female empowerment.

Carrie has been writing, for an audience, since the age of sixteen and has a BA(Hons) in Communication Studies, specializing in Journalism. It is only recently, through the love of reading, that she has taken up writing again.

She is married with two boys and a cat.

As well as reading she enjoys binge watching crime dramas and growing random plants.

Printed in Great Britain
by Amazon